T0196861

The Lariat

The Lariat

and other writings

JAIME DE ANGULO

EDITED BY DAVID MILLER

COUNTERPOINT

BERKELEY

The Publisher would like to note that eccentric spellings and punctuations reflect Jaime de Angulo's original manuscripts.

Library of Congress Cataloging-in-Publication Data

Angulo, Jaime de.
  The lariat and other writings / Jaime de Angulo ; edited by David Miller.
    p. cm.
  Includes bibliographical references.
  ISBN 978-1-58243-468-1
  I. Miller, David, 1950- II. Title.

  PS3501.N569578L37 2009
  813'.52—dc22

                                2008035705

Cover design by Gopa & Ted2, Inc.
Interior design by Megan Cooney
Printed in the United States of America

Paperback ISBN: 978-1-58243-596-1

COUNTERPOINT
2560 Ninth Street, Suite 318
Berkeley, CA 94710

www.counterpointpress.com

Contents

INTRODUCTION

JAIME DE ANGULO'S WRITINGS have been admired by many other writers over the years, including Ezra Pound, William Carlos Williams, Marianne Moore, Robert Duncan, Allen Ginsberg, and Gary Snyder. Their intrinsic literary merit is, without doubt, one reason for this. However, it is also in the reflection, within de Angulo's writings, of the interconnections between his many activities—as ethnologist and linguist as well as novelist, storywriter, essayist, and poet—that we can best discern his real singularity.

The composer Peter Garland has written of the influence of American Indians and their cultures in de Angulo's creative output. According to Garland, this is one "reason why [his work] is so original and seminal in American letters." He continues:

> What de Angulo's work shows us is that native American music and oral literature provide more than just exotic, "quotational" matter, or flavor; rather they offer new formal models and attitudes towards the material at hand (music or words) . . .

> *. . . Rather than emulating the "sound" of Indian music or poetry, we can use these new attitudes to speak in, and develop, voices that are completely our own. De Angulo's high achievement as an artist was in doing precisely that—and why there is such a thin distinction in his work between the ethnological and the creative.*[1]

If Garland's emphasis is mainly on de Angulo's poetry and musical notations—neither of which are represented in this selection, which focuses on his prose—his point is generally valid.[2] In particular, de Angulo's narrative strategies are developed from American Indian storytelling, with a characteristic interplay of given (traditional) material and individual improvisation, and informed by American Indian mythology. At the same time, he is capable of utilising European narrative models—as in his novel *The Lariat*—with incursions of elements from American Indian lore and storytelling, to considerable effect.

De Angulo pursued such unusual work in a way that was uniquely his own, and which still claims our interest and admiration—as well as anticipating much later developments.[3] His knowledge and engagement with American Indian traditions, as well as his willingness and ability to draw on European traditions, have already been mentioned. What needs to be added to this is the sense one often has with his writing—that he is literally *at the edge.* I mean that he is at the edge of different cultures and traditions, and drawing upon either or both; but more than this, his texts *cross over*—from one realm or territory, one culture to another—and back, with an intensity and depth of involvement and realization.

Beyond his writings, Jaime de Angulo's reputation has been based to some extent on the legendary character of his life. In the present context, however, it is more important to look at how he crossed over from one culture, and one discipline or field, to another—not only in his writings, but also in the way he lived his life.[4]

Jaime de Angulo was born January 22, 1887, to a Spanish family living in France.[5] Restless and rebellious from an early age, he left home in 1905. He was in revolt against his bourgeois family, his Jesuit education, and European culture, and seeking to make his fortune. (He denied any rebellion, however, in his communications with his father.) After a series of ill-fated adventures, he arrived in San Francisco the day before the great 1906 earthquake. De Angulo worked as a cowboy and rancher from early in his life in America, and continued in ranching, on and off, in subsequent years. However, he also studied medicine, first at Cooper Union and then at Johns Hopkins, where he met his first wife, Cary Fink.[6]

He became interested in anthropology and American Indian studies in the early 1910s, during a period when a research position in biology at Stanford University was followed by another spell as a rancher. Indeed, it was when he was a cattle rancher in Alturus, Modoc County, California, in 1914, that de Angulo first encountered the Achumawi or Pit River Indians, who would come to be his special interest amongst American Indian tribes. (He was also given the appellation "Buckaroo Doc" around this time, by some of the cowboys he knew in Modoc County. The nickname aptly sums up his unusual combination of activities.)

De Angulo joined the U.S. Army Medical Corps in 1917, and was trained in psychiatry (and was later involved in training others). It was around this same time that he became aware of Jungian psychology. (His wife, Cary, discusses Jung in a letter to de Angulo of February 1918.) De Angulo became more interested in Jungian ideas in the early 1920s, after Cary—who had by this time divorced him but was still in touch—began working with Jung in Zurich. De Angulo visited Zurich in 1923, and had several meetings with Jung.

After his discharge from the Army at the end of 1918, de Angulo—in the company of Lucy (known as Nancy) Freeland—came to know the anthropologists Alfred Kroeber, Paul Radin and Paul-Louis Faye. (Nancy Freeland would later become de Angulo's second wife.) Subsequently, Kroeber invited de Angulo to teach courses on psychology in relation to anthropology at the University of California at Berkeley.

In 1920, de Angulo also developed a fascination with linguistics, and began his first work in field linguistics (with a Pomo Indian, William Benson, who was to become a longtime friend). By this point, most of his major concerns were in place—psychology, anthropology, linguistics, American Indian studies. By September 1921 he was already working on the language of the Achumawi (as related many years later in his memoir *Indians in Overalls*). He would work on numerous American Indian—and Mexican Indian—languages over the years, as well as taking down stories and investigating the way of life and psychology of American Indians.

He made friends with the poet Robinson Jeffers during this same period. Jeffers was his neighbour in Big Sur, where de Angulo had established a ranch a few years earlier. De Angulo appears to have been fascinated by Jeffers as a person, while claiming that he took little or no interest in his poetry.[7]

It is difficult to know when to date many of de Angulo's writings, but by the mid-1920s he had begun to publish fiction as well as essays in various periodicals (ranging from a literary magazine entitled *Laughing Horse* to *Language* and *American Anthropologist*).[8] These early writings include his first novella, *Don Bartolomeo*, a melodramatic tale which in its depiction of conflict between European and American Indian beliefs and ways of thinking, and its concern with powerful passions, foreshadows *The Lariat*, a much more complex and accomplished work of fiction. They also include such important early contributions to American Indian studies as "The Background of the Religious Feeling in a Primitive Tribe" and "On the Religious Feeling Among the Indians of California"—interestingly complementary pieces, one written for an academic journal, the other for a literary "little magazine."

He also met D.H. Lawrence during this period, when Lawrence was staying with Mabel Dodge Luhan in Taos, New Mexico, and de Angulo was visiting—primarily to see Mabel Dodge Luhan's husband, Tony, a Taos Indian. A rivalry seems to have developed between de Angulo and Lawrence. At any rate, de Angulo is distinctly ambivalent about Lawrence in the letters he wrote from Taos.[9]

De Angulo wrote another of his novellas, *The Witch*, while he was in Taos.[10] Mabel Dodge Luhan suggests in *Lorenzo in Taos* that this was out of rivalry with Lawrence—or to impress him. It would have been typical of de Angulo that the writing of this novella may have been provoked by personal rather than strictly literary concerns. He showed little interest in contemporary literature, and his relations with other writers—whether friendly or otherwise—were rarely based on any real knowledge of their writings.[11]

Many of de Angulo's important later writings were first drafted in the 1920s, including *The Lariat* (also known as *The Reata)* and *Indian Tales for a Little Boy and Girl. (Indian Tales for a Little Boy and Girl* was the basis for *Old Time Stories* (his radio broadcasts), *Indian Tales, Shabegok,* and *How the World Was Made.*) However, he continued to be very active in anthropology and linguistics, and he was professionally involved with both Franz Boas and Edward Sapir—highly significant and influential figures in these fields. He also made recordings on wax cylinders of American Indian songs, as well as transcribing them (using a form of notation of his own devising).[12]

Carl Jung visited the States in 1925, and de Angulo took him to meet some Taos Indians. At that point, he was still close to Jung's ideas, but he was subsequently to turn violently against Jung. There were personal grounds for his later feelings about Jung, as well as what he seems to have perceived (and deplored) as pseudo-mystical tendencies in Jungian psychology. (He also goes further, and refers to Jung as a "charlatan.")[13]

It is impossible to understand de Angulo's later years without mentioning the death of his young son Alvar in a car crash in 1933.[14] It would not be an exaggeration to say that his psychological state was precarious, and his behaviour frequently extreme in the years following this tragic occurrence.[15] His family life suffered as a result: de Angulo's marriage to Nancy broke down, and his relations with his daughter, Gui, were difficult right to the end of his life. However, it is also true that de Angulo's commitment to his writing increased from this time on; as well as rewriting older work, he wrote new pieces, such as the novella *The Androgynes*, and *Indians in Overalls*. He also developed a remarkable body of poetry.[16] Although he was no longer interested in field research in linguistics, he worked on a theoretical book called *What is Language?*[17]

It was at the end of 1948, when de Angulo was in the hospital for treatment of prostate cancer, that he began to correspond with Ezra Pound. A neighbour of de Angulo's in Big Sur, Hugh O'Neill, had thought that the two men, both in hospitals (in Pound's case, a psychiatric hospital), could do with the contact. Characteristically, de Angulo admitted to Pound that he had never read any of his work! Pound and his wife Dorothy both gave him a great deal of encouragement with his writing, and it was through the Pounds that *Indians in Overalls* appeared—remarkably, in its entirety—in *The Hudson Review*.[18] It is highly likely that it was also through Ezra Pound's recommendation that the poet Peter Russell published de Angulo's "Don Gregorio" (as well as his translation of Federico Garcia Lorca's poem "Arqueros") in *Nine*. De Angulo was also in contact with the poets Jack Spicer and Robert Duncan. In fact, Duncan lived in the same house as de Angulo for a while, and acted as his typist.

He received further encouragement when he was asked to broadcast his retellings (supposedly for children) of American Indian stories, which he called *Old Time Stories*, over the Berkeley radio station KPFA, beginning in spring 1949.[19] This material was reshaped as *Indian Tales*, which de Angulo said "helped [him] to see deeper than ever into the significance of mythology."[20] The Pounds eventually found a publisher for *Indian Tales*—unfortunately, three years after de Angulo's death from cancer in October 1950.[21]

"I want to know [about American Indian lore] because I think the whites have lost their soul and they must find it again," de Angulo said. "Some of the things the whites have lost, the Indians have kept."[22] Elsewhere he wrote: "In Europe we can go back to our mother the earth through the spirits of our own ancestors. They inhabit the soil, the trees, the rocks. In America the soil is teeming with the ghosts of Indians. Americans will never find spiritual stability until they learn to recognise the Indians as their *spiritual* ancestors."[23]

De Angulo's sense of displacement from his own European culture was significant—for himself and for his writings. This is especially true with regard to religious belief. How much de Angulo interpreted American Indian beliefs according to his own need to find something as far removed as possible from the religious beliefs he had grown up with is open to debate. What is less in dispute is the extent to which he formed a special attachment to the Achumawi as the tribe whose beliefs seemed to him the farthest from Judeo-Christian religion.

Yet de Angulo's background was very definitely European—he came from a Spanish family, his formative years were spent in France, and he was Jesuit-educated. (He writes engagingly about some aspects of this background in "Don Gregorio.") Also, he can be described as (amongst other things, at least) a Western intellectual involved in scientific field research.[24]

I tend to think that de Angulo was in many ways able to fit in with European and white American modes of thinking and social circles, and similarly able to fit in with American Indians—while remaining in some respects "apart" in both cases. D.L. Olmsted, in the introduction to his *Achumawi Dictionary*, comments that de Angulo "pursued his work under difficulties: his change of country and language; his change of research interest and profession; his lack of a regular academic connection; his lack of any regular training in linguistics."[25] (It's also worth recalling de Angulo's own comment on his relationship to the academic community: "Decent anthropologists don't associate with drunkards who go rolling in ditches with shamans.")[26] I think it is also clear from de Angulo's own account in *Indians in Overalls* that he was both accepted to a large degree by the American Indians he met and lived with, yet was also something of an outsider. Again, I can't help feeling that this situation—with regard to both his fellow anthropologists and linguists, and the American Indians he knew—contributed to the particular quality of his dialogue with American Indian culture.

As the texts in this book show, there is a considerable diversity to de Angulo's writing—from the humorous, impressionistic sketches that constitute "Don Gregorio," to the informal memoir "First Seeing the Coast," and the essay "The Background of the Religious Feeling in a Primitive Tribe." As much as anything, however, it is de Angulo's ability to powerfully realise his fascination with American Indian mythopoeia in such texts as "The Gilak Monster and his Sister the Ceremonial Drum" and "The Fury of Loon Woman," which impresses and engages. He doesn't treat this material as "exotic" but more meaningfully in terms of an alternative way of thinking—what he calls the "meta-logical thinking" of mythology—and its relation to emotional, psychological, and spiritual aspects of existence.[27]

"The Gilak Monster and his Sister the Ceremonial Drum" is a retelling of a Pomo Indian story, and was included in the radio broadcasts de Angulo made for KPFA. It is hence oral in derivation and oral in intention, yet also extremely visual in its written version. (It is also a good example of his poetic approach to language.) De Angulo is often surprising and paradoxical. He is also inventive, audacious, playful . . . and much more.[28] He crosses boundaries, he deals in alternatives, he is both a sceptical, scientific European and an enthusiastic, engaged witness to American Indian storytelling and spirituality. He was the sort of person apt to roll around drunkenly in ditches with shamans.[29] He is a writer of singularity and importance.

The Lariat

Don Gregorio

Don Gregorio and the Straw Hat

That summer we were vacationing in Trouville, which in those days of the mid 90's was a fashionable seaside resort. My father's current fad at that time was the Kneip Cure, which enjoyed a great vogue in those days among the devotees of health and rational living. One of the tenets of the Cure was to eat slowly and chew the food thoroly - in fact you shud masticate every morsel no less than a dozen times before swallowing it. My father took this, as everything else, literally; there he sat at his meal, with his head turned sideways to the open book of the moment, conscientiously masticating each piece twelve times. He ate alone, and his meal lasted from five to seven o'clock. The rest of the family, my mother, my sister, my brother and I, trooped in at six o'clock and were finished by half past six. My father was never able to make any of us masticate properly, altho he tried.

Another tenet of the Cure was to walk barefoot in the grass before the morning dew had evaporated. This, my father did every morning. Both he and I were early risers, always up at dawn (I was about six or seven, then). So we sallied forth, both barefoot, and walked a mile or so out of town to where there were some lush green cow pastures, he walking ahead with his long strides and I trotting behind like a faithful dog.

My father never wore a hat. In those days a hat was as necessary a part of a man's costume as were his trousers, and to go about bareheaded was as unusual as to go about without his pants, and almost as shocking. But my father cared not a fig for public opinion (to which he referred, contemptuously, as *la vanidad mundana);* he did not affront it; he did not ignore it; he simply did not see it. He never realized that he was an odd, an eccentric character. But my poor mother did! Dona Ysabel was a paragon of conventional correction (or maybe we thot so because of the contrast with Don Gregorio?).

That summer, however, my father was much bothered by the glare of sunlight; and on that particular morning, as we were returning on bare feet from those dewey meadows, he made an important decision: he wud buy a straw hat!

So, we turned into the town in quest of a hat-shop. The morning was just getting along and people were leisurely shopping here and there. We found a hat shop and went in. There was a demoiselle behind the counter and my father explained in his grammatically correct but atrociously pronounced French that he desired a straw hat with a very wide brim. The demoiselle smiled and said, "Oui, Monsieur, certainement" and disappeared and soon returned with several trim *canotiers,* those stiff little hats they used to wear in summer in Europe and in New York but I never saw one in the West. My father's face fell. No, no, no, he cried, that was not at all what he wanted (and indeed, he wud have been a figure of fun in one of the little monkey hats, he with his prophet's face and flowing beard!). He wanted a hat with a large brim, a very wide brim.

So the demoiselle went back and returned with some more *canotiers*... the brim of these was surely all of a quarter-inch broader, in fact they were daringly wide brimmed.... Just then, my father's eye lit on a pile of gardener's hats put away on a top shelf. "Ha!" he exclaimed triumphantly, that was what he wanted.

The demoiselle's eyes were wide with horror. "Mais, Monsieur, ce sont des chapeaux de jardinier!" (Now, observe: she said they were gardener's hats, not garden hats. A tremendous difference in social classification!) My father's answer was "It is all equal to me! I want one of those hats! Give me one of those hats!" She climbed on a short ladder and she brot them down. I thot she was going to burst into tears. As a final plea to my father to be reasonable, she said: "But Sir, they cost only six pennies!" "Eh bien, tant mieux! all the better!" said my father and he crowned himself with a gardener's hat. He really did not look bad at all in it. It fitted his noble face. The demoiselle's look of on-the-verge of tears changed to a slightly admiring one. But my father's eternal utilitarianism had to spoil the picture again. He demanded to have ribbons sewed on to the hat so he cud tie them under his chin against the wind. Now the demoiselle's smile changed to plain laughter. She rummaged under the counter and produced scissors, needle and thread, and a wide red ribbon. In a few deft movements she had two ribbons sewed on to the hat; my father crowned himself again; and she herself tied the scarlet bow-knot under his beard. She was laughing. Her laughter did not at all annoy my father. He simply remarked to me: "Pero, que amable es!"

And we sallied forth into the street, my father barefoot and with his new hat, and me trotting behind him.

We were now going home, and there were quite a few people on the streets. Just then, coming in our direction, but on the other side of the street, we saw my mother. Dona Ysabel was short and somewhat corpulent; tightly laced in her corsets and wearing very high heels; she always dressed carefully in the correct mode of the day, but without any ostentation. So there she came as usual walking very erect with her short steps, holding her train in one hand and her parasol in the other. As I said, we saw her; *and she saw us at the very same instant.* She stopped abruptly for perhaps five seconds. Then she whirled around, and fled up the street.

"Ysabel! Eh... YSABEL!!!" my father yelled in stentorian tones, taking long strides.

Passers-by stopped and turned around, staring, and shop-keepers came to their doorsteps. "Ysabel, Eh, Ysa-BEL!!" But Dona Ysabel was fleeing up the street, almost at a run. At the corner she turned into another street. My father stopped. He turned to me. "Pero, que le pasa, esta loco (what is the matter with her? is she crazy?)."

DON GREGORIO'S BANDOLEER

My father hated pockets. He said they were illogical (why? asked my mother, and he answered: you don't understand) and unsightly, and they deformed the clothes (that from him!) and bulky (but why do you have to carry a department store along with you? you don't need all that truck, tantas cositas!). So he had his tailor make him special clothes *without* pockets, and he carried all his cositas in a bandoleer. Women do the same nowadays, but when I was a child, women used neither bandoleer nor handbag, nor did they have pockets to their clothes (except a dissimulated placket situated in the slit of the skirt, just beneath the bustle - and of course quite invisible since in walking a lady gathered her train in her right hand and held it off the ground by bunching it under her posterior).

In that placket she carried her money-purse. Her handkerchief she carried in her sleeve. That's all a lady need carry in those days (I haven't mentioned the umbrella, or parasol - according to the weather of the day - held in the left hand, but it goes without saying it). In those days only the prostitutes painted their faces or lips, or a few old ladies who had been known for their beauty when they were young, and now they couldn't accept their fate. At most it was permissible, and only in a woman "entre deux ages", to powder her face (but very lightly, just enough to hide the lines) - and perhaps, perhaps to do something to her eyes, but so carefully, so well, that it defied detection. Anything more was "maquillage" and only for the cocottes. As for a woman to make her face in the public eye - as they do now in restaurant, streetcar, anywhere - it wud have been as shocking as if she had lifted her skirts to squat, or almost.

Now, in that bandoleer he carried an assortment of things, to-wit:

1. 3 pairs of spectacles: one for near vision, one for far vision, and one that combined both far and near.

2. a pencil.

3. his "breviary", for my father who was very pious, read the holy offices every day, like an ordained priest.

4. his rosary of beads.

5. a bunch of slips of paper on which was printed his name and address; these he collected by cutting out the paper-band wrapper around the newspaper to which he subscribed. My father considered calling cards one of the "mundane vanities". Anyway, Don Gregorio was one of those people who are called penny-wise and pound-foolish. He saved every piece of string, carefully rolling it up like a diminutive reata, and storing it away in a drawer. Likewise he opened envelopes and saved them for scribbling paper. (But when we went to the country for the summer vacation, we travelled in a private railroad car! And that's how he went through the million or so in francs that belonged to my mother in about twenty years time and was practically a pauper in his old age. Don Gregorio, Don Gregorio de las Cositas, we used to call him, penny-wise and pound-foolish, so logical and so naïve. He was quite unlike anybody I ever knew... but to come back to the cositas in that bandoleer:

6. his money-purse.

7. a pen-knife.

8. a compass (what for, in Paris?).

9. his second chronometer (I mean the no. 2 pocket-chronometer; the ship-chronometer of course never left the house!).

10. four handkerchiefs, big handkerchiefs, in colored plaids, like glorified bandannas, but of linen (glorious things, but

you can't get any such things any more). One of these four handkerchiefs was for nose-blowing (altho Don G. almost never blew his nose. "I have no secretions!" he said proudly). The second handkerchief was for wiping his spectacles. The third kerchief was for opening doors when out of the house (Don Gregorio had caught the microbe phobia - this was not so very long after Pasteur and Metchnikoff, and microbes were the current fad - those terrible MICROBES of my childhood! Los microbios, los microbios! Alli vienen los Moros!...) As for the 4th and ultimate handkerchief, we never learned its use or purpose. When questioned about it, Don G. wud never answer, but merely smiled, as if to say: "Este es mi secreto!"

Don Gregorio at the Bon Marché

My father cud at times turn into quite an orator, and this was all the more surprising in a man ordinarily so silent. Unfortunately, his gifts of oratory were usually spent on us children. We wud be summoned into the presence by our rings....

But I must explain about the rings. When Don Gregorio wanted to communicate with his family, he rang (if we were at the time in our Paris apartment; but in our country-house he used a whistle, like a boatswain on board ship). For Dona Ysabel the signal was two long rings; for my sister Pura, one long and one short; for Manuel, one long and two shorts, and for myself one short and two longs. So, when we heard rrrrring-ring, then rrrrrring-ring-ring, and then rrrrring-ring-ring-ring it was like a general alarm, and we knew we were in for a lecture. We wud troop into Don Gregorio's cabinet-de-travail and stand in a row in front of his desk where he sat reading a book, or perhaps writing, and we waited for his clearing-of-the-throat. This was akin to the regulation three knocks that preceded the raising of the curtain on the stage. Hrmmm, hrmmm, hrmmm.... Then he wud rise and stand up on his chaufferette, that footwarmer - a flat box with a copper lid and a little wick oil-lamp inside - which he carried around with him all over the place everywhere in the apartment because his feet were always cold; and that made him stand a little over six feet. Now he plunged into the exordium. It might start something like this: "Hrmmm, hrmmm, hrmmm... Order is a great quality. It is perhaps the greatest gift from God to man. Without order, the world is nothing but a hodge-podge (sin orden, el mundo no es mas que una sinrazon). With order..." and so on and so forth, thru the main body of the discourse to the final peroration... to the final peroration, that is, *if* no accident occurred. Jaime was usually the accident because as a child he was tempestuous and impatient, and he might break out with: "Yes, I know, it's that blue pencil I took out of the drawer (the second drawer on my father's bureau, on the right hand, where he kept colored pencils and saved-up little rolls of string), but I'll go and fetch it..." then my father wud give me a withering glance (and his blue eyes cud be very piercing, at times), and with great dignity, but without any heat, he said: "Silencio!... *Vuelvo a repetir*" and he wud start again at the very beginning; "Order is a great quality; it is perhaps the greatest..." and so on and so forth. How ever many times interrupted he never lost his temper, but only said "Silencio!... Vuelvo a repetir!" and start all over again. There was only one exception. Sometimes we wud be seized by an acces de fou rire, that hysterical laughter without reason. On such occasions my father did not start again at the very beginning. He merely sat down, took up his book, and waited for composure to return to us. Then he wud get up, stand on his chaufferette and resume the lecture at the very point where he had left off, and continue till the end of the peroration.

But I was going to tell about Don Gregorio and the Bon Marché. In those days of my childhood the Louvre and the Bon Marché were the two great department stores. In those stores the system of making purchases was thoroly French and complicated. With the help of a clerk you selected your article, but you didn't pay him for it; he gave you a slip and armed with this slip you went to the comptoir, and took your place in the queue. Then when your turn came to appear before another clerk who sat at the comptoir behind a grille, you presented your slip, paid for the purchase, and received another slip which you presented at the delivery counter where you received your purchase, in case you wanted to take it home with you - but if you wanted it to be delivered at your house, then you said: "a domicile", and gave your name and address to the clerk.

But my father always had trouble with his name and address, because of his foreign accent. So he always carried a provision of those bands that are used in France to wrap around your newspaper. Your name and address are printed on them. As Don G. wud not countenance calling-cards (because he considered them a mundane vanity) he carefully - but several years later he relented. Then he had large bristol-boards, four inches square, engraved ("at least", he said, "if I want to write a message, I will have enough space") he had several thousand of these engraved, for "reasons of economy"; they were of three kinds: Monsieur de Angulo, Madame de Angulo, and Monsieur et Madame de Angulo. The second kind my mother carefully hid, then threw away; the third kind, my father cud never again find, in spite of all his searching thru the drawers of his bureau, but I don't think my mother threw those away - I think she merely misplaced them very carefully - he carefully cut out those bands, and saved them, and carried a little stack of them in his bandoleer. Then when he had to furnish his name-and-address to any one, he wud gravely dig into the bandoleer, and hand over the wrap band cut from the newspaper-wrap. He did this with great dignity, even a sort of flourish, while my mother hovered in the vicinity, and pretended not to know him (we children did not care, rather enjoyed it).

Usually it worked, and the clerk merely scribbled the information on his blotter.

But on this occasion, it did not work as usual.

The clerk was a man with a sallow complexion, a very sallow complexion indeed. When he asked the stereotyped question: "votnoeadres" my father handed him one of the slips. The clerk gave it a passing glance, then threw back the original question at my father. My father did not answer. He merely stuck the slip right under the nose of the clerk. The clerk pushed it aside, and fairly shouted at my father "Kekseksbout-de-papier? J'vous demande vot' nom-et-adresse."

Then the homily started. My mother was pretending to look at some articles on a counter, but her face was red as a tomato. The clerk's complexion had turned from sallow to livid. Customers were staring. A floor-walker tried to intervene but my father said to him a formidable "Silencio." We children were enjoying ourselves hugely. We had been thru so many of these orations!

This time the lecture was all about the rights of the public and the good sense for business to show unfailing courtesy to the customer - a theory generally accepted in America, but not prevalent in France.

The peroration, however, I regret to say, was marred by a touch of argumentum ad hominem. Don Gregorio had finished; he let a slight pause elapse; then he added a postscript: "And anyhow, you are bilious, as anyone can see from your complexion." Unfortunately, like many Spaniards, Don G. got his b's and v's thoroly mixed, and what he said was: "Et d'ailleurs, bous etes Vilieux; cela se boit a botre teint!" Then he marched off, followed in procession by all of us, altho Dona Ysabel was lagging quite a distance behind.

DON GREGORIO AND HIS CHRONOMETER

My father had always had a passion for watches. Yes, a passion! not just an interest, but a passion. Shortly before his death when after 20 yrs. of estrangement I had decided it was stupid on my part to continue the feud, and went and made my submission he said: "I don't remember when this passion started... it must have been during my childhood... the idea that you could, so to speak, materialize time (that most immaterial thing) and metamorfoze it into a maze of wheels inside a little box...."

He kept his watches as other people keep a stable of horses. Usually, watch fanciers are interested in the face of the watch, its style, Ier. Empire, Restoration, Rococo, etc. They keep those watches under cloche and let them run down. Not so with Don Gregorio. He had about three score watches and *they all ran!* He kept them in a closet with shelves. If you were not forwarned and opened the door of the closet you almost fell over backward! Such a racket! Such a tintamarre! Sixty watches ticking at the same time!

Then, on every floor of our villa in La Baule there was one or two of those horloges bretonnes, 6ft. tall. They had a pendulum and a couple of weights. You wound the weights every two weeks. Those were very ornamental clocks. But Don Gregorio did not care a rap about that. The looks of a clock did not interest him; what he wanted was that it shud give the time properly.

But the king of them all was THE chronometer. It was a marine chronometer, one of those things in a box about a foot square, and hung so that it was always level. It had been made by Leroy-Beaulieu, the great chronometer-maker of the Bould. de la Madeleine. Don Gregorio had paid a fortune for it! Naturally, you never changed it. You simply calculated each time the amount it had gained or lost. A good chronometer does not vary more than seven seconds a day. But the really important thing is that it should vary (either advance or retard) a regular amount. A chronometer which gains a second one day, then three the next, then retards one second the next day, is not a good chronometer; too temperamental!

In those days before wireless, my father got the *right* time from the Navy, at Saint-Nazaire some 20 kilometers from La Baule. My father made the trip every 2 weeks, by train, just to obtain the right time. He carried in his sack a small quasi-chronometer and this he put in accord with the Chronomètre de la Marine. He always went alone except that I accompanied him. I adored my father the way one adores God. If I had had my way I wud never have left his side. He never even noticed my presence, and he never said anything to me. He was one of the most silent men I have ever known; at least in those days he was.

I pause here a moment for a query: *why* was Don G. so much in love with watches? As I have said already, it was not the artistic value of the watch; that left him completely indifferent. Neither was it the *collector's instinct.* My father collected many items that usually go into collections; at various times he collected lenses, pictures, rocks, meteorites (that was when we were in the Pyrénées - and the peasants, the montagnards, collected them in the high mountains and then sold them to the tourists - but always after breaking them in half to show the beautiful shining structure of the metal - to my father this was sacrilege!

he wud buy none of those, to the amazement of the peasants - he tried vainly to explain to them that these ugly objects came *from another planet than* the earth, they came from outer space - mais vas donc leur faire comprehendre, ces pauvres imbéciles! They looked at my father with suspicion). He collected Moorish plates. Postage-stamps are the only thing he never collected, strangely enuf! So, Don Gregorio *did* have the instinct of a collector, there is no denying it. Yet I was certain, even far back in the days of my childhood that the collector's instinct had nothing to do with it. I was puzzled - and I did not understand it until years later, just before his death.

So I quarreled with him and came to America and had no more communication with him until years later when I realized that I was acting like a fool and went back and made my submission, and he died happy.

Now, the story of my father, his valet-de-chambre and the chronometer happened some ten years later, during the First World War. (I volunteered in the medical corps, 1st Lieut. and spent the next 18 months trying to find out *where I was supposed to be!* The Army had misplaced my papers. It's incredible but it is so!) So, I never was present at the "Affaire du Chronomètre". All I know is what my Sister told me.

Altho my father hardly ever spoke to anyone his figure was well-known in the country-side where he took long rides on his bicycle. They thot he was a sort of madman, but quite harmless. "Le millionaire espagnol" they called him. Somehow or other the idea had entered his head that he had been appointed official time-keeper for the county. He had taken it upon himself to care for the great church clock on the main square of the town. He had also taken charge of the clock at the railway-station. And whenever he met someone in uniform, the postman maybe, or a garde-champêtre, he offered to give them the correct time. The transaction was a silent one - no words wasted. Don Gregorio took his watch out of his pocket and the other person did the same. They compared the watches side-by-side; the small error, if there was one, was corrected and each man went his way, smiling.

All this was before the days of the radio. The radio changed Don Gregorio's life. No longer necessary, those bi-weekly trips to Saint Nazaire to get the proper time at the Bureau de la Marine. Now he cud have the correct time *twice* a day, at noon and at midnight. Incredible! Life was good.

The war! and the American troops occupied Brittany and went joyously at the game of teaching the Frogs the ways of the superior life. All private radios were, of course, ordered dismantled. But now that he had tasted the intoxicating thing, he cud not face going back to the old life. *He decided to take a chance!* He would keep his antenna. Nobody wud notice. The childish lack of appreciation of reality is appalling! It also showed an appalling lack of understanding of war and the military mind. Because he was so certain of his honesty he thot that honesty wud immediately become apparent to the others. My sister was in tears!

It did not take the occupying Americans long to discover my father's radio, and they demanded Don Gregorio's arrest as a spy. In vain did the French authorities plead with the American commander. "The man is well-known to us - absolutely harmless - just a crackpot - ." The American was obdurate.

Now things began to move fast - everybody moved fast except Don Gregorio. He was sublimely ignorant of the danger. He had done no wrong, he was quite serene. But it was the hour of his lunch when they came to arrest him, and he refused to move until he had had his lunch. In vain the Commissaire de Police appealed to him. "Monsieur, je vous en prie, pressez-vous, pressez-vous, vous n'avez pas l'air de comprehendre la situation. Vous entendez ces cris, dehors? Eh bein c'est la foule en émeute. Vous n'avez probablement jamais vu une foule en émeute. Moi, c'est mon métier. Ce sont de braves gens qui tout à coup deviennent des bêtes-en-fureur."

My sister told me that it was one of the most terrible moments of her life. "Figurez-vous cette foule, d'ordinaire de bons paysans, des commerçants polis, des voisins aimables. Et tous hurlaient 'A mort l'espion! L'espagnol à la lanterne, l'espagnol à la lanterne!'" And between them and the grille of the garden, some twenty mounted policemen with slung carbines. In the salle-à-manger Don Gregorio eating an omelette with perfect unconcern, served by the butler in civvies (they had arrested him as accomplice).

Finally the omelette was finished and the three of them descended the stairs and entered the police wagon. The mounted policemen quickly formed an escort around the wagon, and off they went for the railroad station. The way led past the Place de l'Eglise. The Commissaire told my sister that Don Gregorio begged them to stop so he cud put the big clock on time.

The Americans kept Don Gregorio and the butler in jail for a whole month before they were convinced of his innocence. Don

Gregorio and the butler had to share the same cell. Don Gregorio kept up a jeremiad of self-accusatory acts of contrition. It was God punishing him, and that sort of thing. Eugène at first assented "Oui Monsieur, oui Monsieur." Then he became surly and did not open his mouth any more. Then one day, in the midst of a jeremiad he got up deliberately from his cot, he bent over and took hold of the pot-de-chambre in both hands, and he stood over Don Gregorio: "Un mot de plus... et je vous mets la tête en bouillie!" My father yelled: "Au secours. 'il est devenu fou!" After that they were put in two separate cells.

Years after, when I visited him and my sister, I found them in the Basque country, on the French side. He had changed very much, of course, mellowed. My sister explained to me that she could not bear living in La Baule after the trouble. The place has become odious to her. "Je n'oublierai jamais le cauchemar de cette foule hurlant. 'A mort l'espion! l'espagnol à la lanterne!' Ces têtes défigurées par la cruauté, par une passion obscène!" She had sold the house for a song and they had come here to the lovely Pays Basque.

One evening, my father and I sat outside smoking. The night was warm and clear, and the stars brilliant. My father began telling me how he had managed to get the right time before private radios were allowed again. He had made friends with one of the French priests at a local astronomical observatory. He had learned to calculate "sidereal time" by making observations on the stars. And with emotion choking his voice he told me how he had discovered a new world! "Just think, just think about the speed of light, 200,000 kilometers per second!" His voice had dropped to a murmur. He began to tell me about the wonders of modern physics. Then he told me how time was only one of the four coordinates of matter... *Then it was that I understood his passion for watches.*

The night-chill entered into us and we went indoors. It was almost midnight and time for the broadcast of the time from the Eiffel tower. And while we waited for it a strange expression came over his face. "They* wanted me to study law! I never understood the law! For me it was only a jumble of illogicalities, a senseless galimatias! Just suppose they had let me learn physics and chemistry, biology - I might have become a great scientist! But Spain is a barbarous country!" and while he was saying that, a wave of bitterness was swelling inside myself. I wanted to say: "Yes, and you my father kept me in schools of Jesuits where we were forbidden to read books on physics and chemistry, and biology!" but I did not say it.

Pretty soon the signals began coming in. The large room was very dimly lit by an oil-lamp, one of those things in the Pyrénées that have not changed since Roman times. You still find them in use. It looks like half of an avocado pear, with a wick which dips in the oil (olive oil was so cheap in those days!) the wick hangs outside and it gives out a soft yellow light. The room was full of dancing shadows.

Now the signals were coming fast and Don G. was entering them in notebooks for the several chronometers (of the 2nd class), and to his horror one of them that he was especially interested in

---

*By "they" he meant the Jesuits. He had been one of their brilliant pupils.

had gone on a rampage! It was several seconds off (we discovered the next day that it was my father who had made a mistake!).

I started for my room and turned around to say good-night. My father was sitting in his chair, a picture of desolation. He held the chronometer in his hand and was shaking his head slowly, from side to side. He was saying in an injured tone "Ay tu, bribon! bribon!" ("oh, you, scoundrel, scoundrel!").

"Marceline, Vous Êtes Une Cochonne!"

For some reason my mother nursed me herself. Just the same, when I was born they sent for a nurse, a "dry nurse". This was Marceline, and she stayed with us until I was six, when she went back to her "pays"; she came from central France.

Marceline was a typical peasant: obdurate, stupid, slow (my father nicknamed her Culo-de-Plomo). Naturally she became devoted to me and I became devoted to her. In a sense, she was "mother" to me much more than my mother. Yet, note this point: she addressed me as "Monsieur Jaime", never as plain Jaime; and of course, she used the "Vous."

I can see us going out after lunch, my sister aged 9, my brother 7, and myself 4, all in the charge of Marceline. We go up the Champs-Elysees, around the Arc-de-Triomphe, then we enter the Avenue du Bois (de Boulogne), and before we have gone very far we find some of our "gang" (my sister and my brother are always the leaders, everywhere, it is they who organize games); I hate children, so I stay with "Culo-de-Plomo" who has joined the other bonnes d'enfants on a bench, I play by myself making sand-pies.

Now, for a long time I had been wondering about the jets d'eau of the Place de la Concorde. *What made the water go up?* I used to wonder and wonder and wonder. I lay in bed at night imagining a complicated system of paddle wheels each one throwing some water up to the paddle above, and so on and on. But I knew intuitively that there was something simpler than that!

I asked Marceline. She said she did not know. I insisted that she did. "Tell me, tell me! I want you to tell me!" I got myself into a fury. I stamped my foot. I yelled "Marceline, vous êtes une cochonne!!" to which she replied with calm: "Je le sais. Vous me l'avez dejà dit! ...vous êtes une vieille cochonne!!"

How that problem of artesian water worried me.

It was 2 or 3 years later that I understood, partly. I was playing in the pantry. I had let the water half fill the sink and I was doing something with a little boat I had carved. I don't remember what it was that I was doing but it involved a long rubber tube. Any way, at a certain moment I let the end of the tube drop; the tube had been full of water, and one end of it was still in the sink. I saw the water run out of the other end onto the floor of the pantry and I expected that all the water already inside the tube would thus run out, but to my amazement the water *continued* to run out... and more, and more... and more until *all* the water in the sink had been siphoned out!

We soon heard from the people in the apartment below: their ceiling was leaking! Hulaballoo!! the concierge was there in no time, and the servants from below, and my mother and my brother and sister. They were all trying to find out from me what it was that I was trying to do. But I was like one in a trance!

I knew confusedly in my mind that there was an answer to my great puzzle: what made the water go up. I cudn't work it out but somehow, intuitively, I knew that the two phenomena were connected, the jets d'eau of the Place de la Concorde and the water siphoned out of the sink.

I was angry, I felt cheated. Why didn't they explain important things to little boys?!!

Yes, I was angry, I thot to myself: "yes, at school you fill me up with stupid stories, with arguments about sin, about the state of grace, all sorts of things which bore me, things which I don't understand (and which, I suspect, you do not understand either)! Meanwhile you let a miracle, a real miracle, go bye, and you do not tell me! a miracle which makes me dance with joy, the miracle of communicating vases, the miracle of water going up-hill! Either you have no imagination, or you are very stupid."

Yes, I was angry; I felt cheated; I felt they had let me down. And I wanted to shout: "Vous êtes des cochons! vous êtes des cochons!" I was around 8 or 9. I made my final rebellion when I was just turned 12. I remember that date because it was when I made my "first communion" - a gala day for most boys, but for me a day of disillusion, a day of bitterness. The whole thing, then, was a farce. I cud no longer believe my parents, my teachers. I was on my own; if there is a Truth then I must find it by myself - I was alone, and I was scared. Six long years of loneliness, of bitterness, of doubt - until I broke away and came to America.

First Seeing the Coast

IT WAS SAM SEWARD who first told me abaut the Big Sur country. Sam taught English and literature at Stanford. He had
just returned from a ten-day hike on foot from Monterey in the
north to San Luis Obispo in the south. "You never saw such a
landscape!" he had said, "I did not imagine it was possible... like
a dreamland, somewhere, not real... imagine: only a trail, for a
hundred miles, bordering the Ocean, but suspended above it a
thousand feet, clinging half-way up the side of the sea-wall, and
that wall at an incredible angle of forty-five degrees, a green wall
of grass (he had seen it in winter - throughout the summer the
green is brown-yellow) and canyons with oaks, redwoods, pines,
madronyos, bluejays, quail, deer, and to one side the blue ocean
stretching away to China, and over all that an intense blue sky
with eagles and vultures floating abaut... and nobody, no humans
there, solitude, solitude, for miles and miles - why! in one place
I walked thirty miles between one ranch and the next! - what a
wilderness, what beauty, it's a dreamland, you must go there...."

I somewhat discounted the lyricism of a professional litera-
teur (although I found it subsequently to be all of what Sam had
promised, and more!), still my curiosity was aroused, all the more

so because I was looking for a place in the country where to settle and raise cattle and horses.

I said to Sam: "Why should the country have remained so wild?" "I think it is because when the first expedition was sent out of Mexico with Portolá to rediscover Monterey, they traveled along the sea-shore all the way up to San Luis Obispo, and a little beyond; well, there were about a hundred Spaniards and Indians and two or three hundred horses and pack-animals - quite an expedition to tackle a totally unknown country without roads or even trails! ...and I imagine when they got into that tangle and labyrinth of mountains that fall plumb into the ocean without even a beach, they just got discouraged, and tried going around that clump of mountains; they turned east away from the sea, and found the Salinas valley which led them ultimately to Monterey. That first trip of Portolá established the route for the Camino Real and the Missions. Then Monterey became the capital of California Alta and the center of development - and as there was plenty of good flat land around it, north and west, nobody bothered with that rough land to the south."

Sam was right. That is why that country was always known to the *paisanos* of Monterey as "la costa del Sur", the coast to the south; a wild, little known land, with two rivers; and these two rivers, naturally, were known as "los ríos al sur", the rivers to the south - and to distinguish them: sur grande and sur chico, the little river to the south and the big river to the south. Then came the Gringos, and that not very felicitous combination of "Big Sur". We still receive an occasional letter addressed to "Big Sewer"!

But to go back to my story. It was around Christmas time of '15, and I was loafing in Carmel (which at that time was not much more than two score houses or so); and one day, as I was riding my horse along the road, I saw two vaqueros on horseback. But these two were real vaqueros, and dressed up for going to town - nothing funny or clownish, but the real old stuff: angora chaps, big rowel spurs that tinkled with the gait of the horse, wide sombreros (but not ridiculous); they were riding half-broken colts with jáquimas and fine horsehair mecates... and were they good-looking, the whole outfit of them, horses, men, and equipment!

Since they were paisanos I needed no introduction, and I stopped them: "Where do you come from?" "Allá, de la costa del Sur, allá lojos al diablo... from the coast to the south, from down there to the devil... we are on our way to town to spend Christmas with our mother." "Is there free land down there?" "Plenty of it, hermano, but too wild, too steep, too far from everywhere... nothing but coyotes and deer...." "Fine!" I said, "that's just what I am looking for.... Will you take me down there, when you go back?"

And that's how I made the acquaintance of El Mocho, as we used to call him (like so many vaqueros he had lost a thumb in the coils of the reata), the best horse-breaker I ever knew, and the most reckless, daredevil plenipotentiary whose laughter could be heard half-a-mile away.

He called for me, a week or so later, one morning, on horseback. And although we started early we did not reach his home, at the very end of the wagon-road, until nightfall. Nowadays, when you average sixty miles an hour on smooth highways, people do not realize what traveling horseback meant. A horse does not walk much faster than a man; I must have owned some hundred and fifty horses in my time - and I can only remember three who averaged a steady six-mile an hour walking gait under the saddle. Such a horse is a benediction on a long trip; you are carried along in bliss. But take a slow poke of a horse under you; you keep urging him, urging him, urging him - at the end of the day you are worn out! I should say that most horses average four miles an hour at a steady walk.

That was the end of the wagon-road. The next morning we started on the TRAIL! I shall never forget my first impression when I saw that Coast. I was aghast. I stood still. I looked and looked. What a panorama. The coast made a gentle curve so that I was able to see it for all of thirty miles or so - a wall of green rising abruptly out of the sea, not really perpendicular but halfway so. Headland succeeded headland, like the wings on a stage. And along that wall, a thousand feet above the ocean, the trail.

"Well, what are you waiting for? Are you bemused? encantado?"

"Yes... estoy emocionado... que hermosura!... yes, this is the country I was looking for."

"Wait, you haven't seen anything yet. Wait until I show you the place I have in mind for you."

So we started again on the trail. But I was not used to such height and I felt dizzy. I had to get off my horse and lead him. We came to a bad place: there had been a slide, there was practically no trail left. But the Mocho never got off his colt. Then the colt lost his footing, went off the trail, and started to plunge down that slide of loose rocks.... My heart was in my mouth.... In all the years I have spent around cowboy camps and horse-ranches, I have never seen a rider like this Mocho... he was off the saddle like lightning, the colt turned a somersault and started to roll down toward the ocean, and the Mocho leaping twenty feet at a time, after him... he managed somehow to get hold of the horse's head by the jáquima and keep him from turning over again. Then they scrambled back to the trail, and we went on.

After some riding we arrived at a cabin and dismounted. That's where I first met Clarence, ex-Mormon, not much over 5-foot but strong as an ox, with the flat voice of the nearly deaf, a little wizened face and a heart of gold - but alas, a rather inconsequential type of mind. He wasn't really a moron; it was rather that his mind did not follow the usual grooves and patterns. He came to live with me later on, and I got to know him quite well and appreciate his intimate knowledge of wild nature. He could make a lot of trouble, though, due to a complete ignorance of the cussedness of human nature - with charming naivete and the best intentions, coupled with a penchant for repeating tales, he finally succeeded in getting the whole Coast embroiled in a mix-up of feuds and counter-feuds that lasted twenty-five years - but that's another story, as the fellow said.

Clarence lived there all alone with a pet pig whom he had trained to sit on a chair at table. He also kept bees. He showed us a small churn he had just made out of a 3-lb can of lard and a few sticks whittled with a pocket-knife. His butter was excellent. We had a cup of coffee with him, and remounted our horses.

We followed the Country Trail again for two or three hours. Hanging on the mountainside, a thousand feet above the ocean, then dipping into a wooded canyon with giant redwoods, oaks, madronyos, maples (maples!); I was struck by the diversity of trees; then out again onto grasslands, the trail curving around these "knees of the gods"; then in again into the next canyon... in, out... in, out....

At last the Mocho said: "Here we go up to the place I have in mind for you to homestead" (he said *esquatar* - a barbaric neologism, from squatter, to squat!!). So we turned off the County Trail and started straight up the mountainside... and I must confess I got dizzy and had to get off my horse and lead him, much to the Mocho's amusement. Another hour's climb, and we were there, sixteen hundred feet above the ocean... but I mean above the ocean - the ocean, the blue Pacific, was there, practically under us (not more than a rifle-shot away), sixteen hundred feet below... and gulls flying, and we looking down on them so far down that they were the size of white pigeons.

What a scene! Yes, I lost my heart to it, right there and then. This is the place for a freedom loving anarchist. There will never be a road into this wilderness... it's impossible! Alas, nothing is impossible to modern man and his infernal progress: they came with bulldozers and tractors before very long, and raped the virgin. Roads and automobiles, greasy lunch-papers and beer-cans, and their masters. And the shy Masters of the Wilderness receded to the depths of the canyadas, and back over the Ridge, into the yet unraped country of the Forest Reserve - but even there they are not safe; the well-meaning Rangers (boy-scouts of the forest, one good deed a day) are opening trails, and "restricted" camping grounds, and you must not smoke or swear. A Guide Book to the Wilderness, complete with figures and estimates! Lo, the untamed, adieu....

The Mocho and I were riding to Monterey. The Mocho said: "You have been speaking about building a log-house. Well, here's the man who will build it for you. You see that man walking over the moor with that long stride? Must be Uncle Al - nobody else walks like that - best carpenter on the Coast with broad-ax and adze - but he is a lunatic of the first water - I'll tell you about him later." And a strange figure he was with his long white hair flying in the wind, white mustache and imperial à la Buffalo Bill, a long walking-staff, and a haversack slung over his shoulder. "Sure I'll build you a log-house, best kind of house, best kind of house, keep a going, keep a going, never stop, never stop, that my motto, yessir that's my motto, keep a going, never stop, I'll be down there next week, bring a crew, bring a crew, can't build a log-house alone, you know, hav to have a crew, need a cook, need a cook...." I interrupted this avalanche....

[Note: The manuscript breaks off at this point. –Ed.]

On the Religious Feeling among the Indians of California

THE RELIGION OF THE Indians of California is an inchoate sort of thing. Perhaps I can best express my meaning by a paradox: you can say either that they have no religion at all or that their whole life is nothing but religion. It all depends on what the connotation of that word, religion, is in one's mind. If it mean the *form*, the pattern, the crystallization of that which is the source of the religious feeling, then there is very little religion to be found among the California Indians, I mean in comparison with the Pueblo Indians, for instance, and their elaborate ritual, the highly developed symbolism of their ceremonies, and a fairly developed cosmogony. Or compare them with the Aztecs and the Maya. Or an even higher stage of development among the Egyptians, the Greek - but why should I say "higher"? I really mean more and more developed as to form, that is, where more and more of the stuff of religion has set into definite psychological moulds. But in this process of setting, of crystallizing, has not the original energy been lost, become dead? No, not dead, but rather should I say, *fixed,* in the same sense that we say: the energy of the sunlight is fixed in the chlorophyl of the plant. The religious energy, (that is a psychological energy), is become fixed in certain rites, in certain symbolisms, available to all who understand the particular technique of that kind of mental process, to be tapped by them from those reservoirs of fixed energy, and to be then released as free energy in their own lives.

But there is a time in evolution when the psychological energy which we call the religious sense has not yet become fixated, crystallized, formalized into the patterns of ceremony and ritual. It is then inchoate, formless, loose and permeates the whole world of perception. And I say that this is the stage of the California Indians, at least of the Achumawi whom I know best, and probably also of the Miwok, and undoubtedly of many other tribes. That is why the Achumawi are my favourite Indians, because they are the most primitive. Already among the Pomo (around Ukiah, in north middle California), for instance, you find a certain elaboration of ritual, definite ceremonies at certain dates of the year, a special technique for doctoring, and almost a priesthood. But among the Achumawi there is nothing of all that. There are practically no ceremonies of any kind and no ritual. Any man is a potential priest or doctor. The whole world is full of "spirit", the trees, the stones, the rivers, are full of it. I say spirit in the singular advisedly. Perhaps I would better say "spirit-stuff." For when we speak of a spirit, we mean a *disembodied* spirit. But this primary antimony does not exist in the Achumawi mind, between spirit and body. I think I will come closer to their conception if I say: an object and its essence. That would be our phraseology to express it. But, of course, even there lies an antimony, for us. The point is that for an Achumawi, an object (animal, stone or man) and its spirit, though not the same are yet not opposed, nor even mutually excluding, not even well differentiated. We might say that they are different aspects, or different manifestations of the same thing, that is all. It is like an unseen, untouched, unsmelled, unsensed world of electrical force. To get into communication with it you must do certain things, "tap the wire" as it were. Ordinarily, in most moments of everyday life it is not felt, not sensed, but it is always there, and any time a certain action, a certain emotion may suddenly throw you into *contact* with it, and then, as Jack Folsom said to me "that mountain talks, and you can hear it, and that stone will be talking to a frog, you can hear all that. It's mostly at night, though, or in daytime when you are alone, way off from camp somewhere."

Jack Folsom is not a literal minded man. I feel pretty certain that by talking he does not mean (to himself) words, words of the Achumawi tongue. And I, not being literal minded myself, never asked him, knowing very well that when confronted with the problem of expressing biologically a psychological phenomenon, he would be as stumped as I find myself.

As I said, one is liable to come into contact with this spirit stuff at any moment of life. For instance, when Jack visited me, he found a stone mortar I had collected, sitting by the fireplace. Immediately he rolled a cigarette and blew smoke into it, to quiet it. "That stone don't know me", he explained. "I am a stranger here, and so I had better talk to him and tell him I have nothing wrong in my mind, so he won't hurt me. There are lots of stones like that in our country up north." We were then in Monterey, and the Achumawi live in the upper northwest corner of California.

"No, of course, we didn't make them. Nobody made them. That's the way they are. And there is lots of power to them. They travel all around the country. You maybe find one in some place today, and you come tomorrow and it's moved off down a ways, perhaps quite far off. Of course we use them to pound acorns and things like that, but those are stones that we know. But when you find a new one, somewhere in the country, you had better leave it alone, unless you are a pretty strong doctor. Those things have got too much power."

I must say here that "doctor" is a word used by the Achumawi when they speak English, to denote what is termed by anthropologists as a "shaman" or "medicine man". But I will speak of this in detail in another connection. I merely want to note that the Achumawi use the word in a very loose sort of way. A doctor is not a definite status. Any man may be more or less of a doctor, that is he may *feel* more or less in contact with the spirit stuff and more or less in possession of "power". That power, that the Indians talk about, we may conceive of it, to carry on our comparison to electrical force, as a sort of force of the same quality. That force, that spirit force is not of itself malign, but it is dangerous to handle because it is so much stronger than the biological world of reality, and if you don't know how to handle it you are liable to destroy your own self. Ordinarily, the spirit stuff has no effect on the world of biological reality, because there is no contact between them. But when the contact is established, then the ordinary laws of nature do not apply any longer, you can't tell what may happen. Unless you are wise and understand that technique, you may come to grief. But if you know enough, if you have enough power yourself, then you may touch and handle that mortar stone, that object shaped curiously, yet not shaped by the hand of man, and yet you will not be hurt, not because your power neutralizes that of the stone, nor yet because you are isolated or *insulated* from it, but rather because you know enough to handle the power that will pass into you, when you touch it; perhaps you will see or hear all sorts of queer things, but you will know what they mean, and it will not make you unhappy or queer.

(The mortars found in the Achumawi territory were evidently made by men of a former culture, "prehistoric Indians" so to speak.)

Of course, a good deal depends on individual circumstances. Once in a moment of great confidence, Jack showed me what he called his "protector". He brought out from a sack where he kept several things, a small bundle. He slowly untied the buckskin string that bound it, and then carefully unwrapped several layers of rags, and inside there nested a white stone smaller than an egg, and shaped somewhat like it. It was evidently an artefact. "A little girl found it on the mountain and gave it to me years ago. I call it my protector. But I *don't know the words for it.* If I did I guess I would have lots of power." And he wrapped it up again carefully. That was a sacred object, loaded with emotion for him and so I did not like to ask any jarring questions. I would have liked to know why he had not been afraid to handle it when the little girl brought it to him.

Another time he was walking along a trail, and there in the dust, far from any water, there was a frog who spoke to him, and told him that he need not worry, that he would win that foot race. "That frog told me he would always help me to win races. I was quite a young man then. I got to be known as one of the fastest racers. I used to win all the races and come in easy without even puffing. It was that frog that was doing it for me."

All these are examples of what we may call the fortuitous, the unexpected contacts with the spirit stuff. But there is an important time in life when such contact is deliberately sought for. (I speak of the men, of course. Women must keep away from the spirit stuff. There is between them and it a mutual incompatibility. This is a new state of affairs. It was not so in the days before, in mythological days, but of all this more anon.) At puberty, then, a young man must deliberately seek contact with the spirits. And when I say deliberately, I don't mean for a moment that he goes after it with joy and zest. The young Achumawi Indian would much rather become a full grown Achumawi man without seeking this terrible contact, if that were possible. But it is not possible. His grandfathers, his uncles get after him. And that includes, for uncles, all the men who are "cousins" to his parents in our terminology, however, "brothers" in the Achumawi terminology. However, only those of his uncles who are much older than he, and are men of reputation and character, interfere in his bringing up. They are after him constantly. "You are growing up. Pretty soon you will be a man. It's time for you to go up to the Mountain."

The Mountain is Wadagsudzi (literally: big-standing-it is), one of the largest blocks of mountain that compose the Werner Range dominating the whole Achumawi territory.

And if there is a thing an Achumawi whether boy or man hates to do it is to leave the wide valleys of sage brush and the plateaux covered with sparse juniper, and go up, especially alone, into the tall, gloomy timber of the mountains; but the young man at puberty must make a practice of running up near the end of the day. He must start when the evening glow sets the top of the mountains afire, and he must run up the slopes, fast, fast, faster than the waning light. Every day the old men keep after him. "If you want to get your ears pierced you must be a man. You must go up the mountain and talk to the spirits. Get up in the morning and take a plunge in the creek, make a hole in the ice if you have to. Don't eat so much. Wait until evening before eating. Go hungry. That's the way a man must be when he wants to talk to the spirits."

Finally a day comes when the young man finds enough courage in his heart to go and face the spirits on the lonely mountain top. There are several lakes, there in the tall timber. In the evening glow the lake is full of fire. An Achumawi Indian named George Fox was telling me his own experiences once. "The lake was full of fire when I got there. It scared me. I was afraid to jump in. I had been afraid all the time to come up. But my father was looked up to as a chief. And besides something told me that the spirits wanted to be good to me. It isn't everyone that is wanted by the spirits. Some fellows have no luck. There is no spirit that wants to protect them. Not that they have done anything wrong, but they just have no luck, that's all. You can't tell why the spirits like you, they just take a fancy to you same as we do for a dog or a horse. Well, when I saw that lake full of fire I was scared. That's when I lost my mind, like I was telling you when you asked me if a fellow did really die when he got his ears pierced." At puberty they pierce the ear lobes of young men. The grandfather or an uncle generally does it, seldom the father. "But I shut my eyes and plunged into it. I guess I died then. Anyway I lost my mind because I don't know what happened. But the spirits got me out of there and put me down on the bank. That's where I was when I came back. Then I saw a deer coming. Right away I knew he was my protector. He came and stopped near me and he said, 'Don't be afraid. I will always protect you. You will be lucky.' And ever since then I have always been lucky. I have been a good gambler and I have always had luck." Gambling among the Indians has not the evil connotation it has among us. Jack Folsom speaking to me of his dead son, said, "He was a fine boy, a good worker, a good gambler." The Gambling Game, also called hand-game and grass-game, is a sort of guessing game, played with bones or sticks etc., concealed in the hand. While playing you sing your own favorite songs, the ones you have found to have most power in attracting and holding the attention of the spirit or spirits that protect you. They give you the luck. Of course you must purify yourself before gambling.

Jack Folsom explained further.

"Some people think I have a real power. There is lots of people around here think so. But I have no real power, I am not a doctor, I have only power for myself, that's all. I am healthy, I am never sick, but I can't cure people. No, I have never tried, but I know I can't. That's because I did not have a complete experience. What do I mean by a complete experience? Well, I mean that it wasn't full, it wasn't complete. I don't know how to explain that, but I know it. That deer just gave me luck for myself, but I can't pass it to others. I know it wasn't complete. For instance, if there is someone sick and there is singing, when they sing the deer song, I feel something coming all over me, I feel kind of dizzy, I feel good - but I don't keel over, I don't lose my mind like I would if I had had a complete experience. And that's why I can't eat deer-meat. Oh no, I don't mean that I am not allowed to eat it, but I just can't keep it. I puke it. People have tried to fool me, several times. They give me deer-meat and call it beef, but every time I have puked it. Now, if I had had a complete experience, then I could eat it all right." (They don't taste so very different, at least to me.)

That's what George Fox told me. I wanted to know more, but unfortunately the people of the hotel where I was stopping discovered that he had taken a bath in my room, and they made a scene to me while he was out at lunch. He never came back and I couldn't find him. I don't know, but probably he heard some of the dispute. He was sensitive. I remember on another occasion he had told how they had sent his two boys to the reservation school. "I don't want them to learn what the white people have to teach them. That's what makes young Indians get smart and get into trouble. Because we are Indians that ain't no reason to take our children away from us. You see, an Indian, he loves his children very much and it makes him feel very bad to lose them." His eyes were filled with tears when he said that.

Jack Folsom never had the nerve to go up to the mountain, when he was a young man. He didn't put it exactly that way, but he said he knew that the spirit did not want him to go, so it was no use going.

Sometimes when a young man comes down from the mountain he remains in a state of insanity for several days. He goes around throwing rocks, breaking branches, howling and singing in lonely places.

Even when a young man has had luck with the spirits, he doesn't tell anyone about it. He does not reveal who his "protector" is, not even to his nearest relatives. But of course they are all watching him, and the next time there is a ceremony, if he "keels over" when they are singing the duck song or the mountain lion song, etc. then they know that is his protector, and in the old days before they had acquired the custom of English names, they would bestow upon him a name that contained some allusion to the animal spirit in question, or some well known episode of his mythical adventures.

The Background of the Religious
Feeling in a Primitive Tribe

O UR ATTENTION HAS BEEN recently called again to the
theory that monotheism is the basis of the religion of the
primitives.

In this connection it may be of interest to note that I have
never been able to find the slightest trace of even the vaguest conception of Godhead among the Pit River Indians of northeastern
California. The Pit River tribe, of which the Adzumawi and the
Atsuge are two of the local groups, are an extremely primitive
people. Indeed, the most salient characteristic of their culture is
the absence of nearly everything: no totemism, no social organization, no secret societies, no religious ceremonies of any kind, no
priesthood, no real tabus. This is an imposing array of negative
traits. On the material side their culture is almost as bare; a bow
and arrows, a flint knife and a rabbit-skin blanket, basketry of
medium quality, but no pottery; for clothes, in winter, mere pieces
of fur wrapped and tied around the body or very coarsely sewn
into a semblance of shape, and in summer, none; no weaving; no
sense of decoration and no development of any art technique; no
agriculture. They lived in winter shut up in enormous communal

houses holding as many as ten families, and in summer they roamed around. They were communal hunters, using the system of battues and pits, rather than individual still-hunting. Although they had no agriculture, they developed to a high point what may be termed the "digging-stick culture"; this implies a vast lore and knowledge of edible roots, seeds, and wild vegetables, in what places they grow best and sweetest, at what precise time they are ripe in each particular meadow or hillside, and then of how to half-cook and cure large provisions of them for the winter.

These few remarks will be enough to give the reader the feeling of the life of these people. If anybody is to be called primitive, they are. Indeed, looked at superficially, they must have appeared to the first white men like a horde of beasts. And were it not for the pejorative implications of such a statement by people as contemptuously ignorant of all the rest of creation as we white men are, I would not at all object to their being called animals. For they are very close to the animal stage, the pre-human, pre-rational stage, in the sense that human may be taken as synonym of the concretion of the superorganic into more and more organized forms of culture. Animals are not imbeciles. There is in the life of wild things in a wild setting a multitude of interactions to which the mind of civilized man is not attuned because it is of necessity oriented to another aspect of mental energy, namely the rational. To understand the psychology of the Pit River people, it is necessary to visualize their extremely intimate contact with the trees, the rocks, the weather and the delicate changes in the atmosphere, with the shape of every natural object, and, of course, with the habits not only of every species of animal but of many individuals. It is almost impossible for a civilized man to form any conception of the degree of intimacy with nature this represents. No civilized man would ever have the patience and energy to loaf in a wild place long enough to catch this subtle rhythm of interactions.

I have said that the Pit River were extremely primitive; I might have said that they still are. For though in the fifty or so years they have been in contact with the whites they have adapted themselves amazingly well to all the material aspects of civilization so that today they dress in overalls, use gasoline engines to saw wood, and ride in Fords, on the spiritual side they have not amalgamated a single one of the white man's values. But, the reader will ask, if they have no religious ceremonies, no priesthood, no ritual of any kind, and not the slightest approach to any conception of Godhead, how can one speak of their having any spiritual or religious values? I grant that it may sound somewhat paradoxical, but I must answer that on the contrary the life of these Indians is nothing but a continuous religious experience. To me, the essential of religion is not a more or less rationalized conceptual system of explanations of reality, but rather the "spirit of wonder", or as Lowie puts it: the recognition of the awe-inspiring, extraordinary manifestations of reality. The difference between the two attitudes is essential. The one leads ultimately from humble origins in explanatory myths and stories of creation to a scientific discipline. The other is the mystical attitude, sufficient unto itself for those who happen to possess it, but an eternal puzzle and source of annoyance to the others because it stubbornly resists all attempts at rationalization.

Therefore, it is logically impossible for the rational man to understand the religious feeling of the primitives, and this is the probable cause of the failure of orthodox scientific ethnology in this field. To try to derive philosophical concepts and systems from the belief in spirits, the recognition of the self in dreams, errors in causal thinking about the phenomena of reality, or any of the other attempts at deriving the religious spirit from something else than itself, will always appear as utterly futile to anyone with a modicum of that spirit of wonder in himself. Unfortunately the man who does not possess it finds himself of necessity driven to explain in terms of his own thinking a phenomenon which he observes in others but which he does not experience himself, a phenomenon, at that, which is essentially subjective but which he endeavours to apprehend by purely objective means. I think this is not only poor philosophy but poor science.

The spirit of wonder, the *recognition of life as power,* as a mysterious, ubiquitous, concentrated form of non-material energy, of something loose about the world and contained in a more or less condensed degree by every object, - that is the credo of the Pit River Indian. Of course he would not put it in precisely this way. The phraseology is mine, but it is not far from their own. Power, power, power, this is the burden of the song of everyday life among these people. Without power you cannot do anything out of the ordinary. With power you can do anything. This power is the same thing as *luck.* The primitive conception of luck is not at all the same as ours. For us luck is fortuitousness. For them, it is the highest expression of the energy back of life. Hence the sacred character of all forms of gambling in primitive life.

There, in gambling, in the "hand-game", you will find the true expression of religious feeling in form, if you are looking for religious form. Watch the fervor of the two teams as they sing the rhythmic songs of power for a whole night and you cannot escape the feeling that gambling here is a religious experience. "My son was a fine boy", said Fighting-in-the-Brush to me once, "he was a steady fellow, a good worker, a good gambler!" And again, here is Likely Ike explaining to me the theology of the so-called Shaker religion of the Klamath Indians among whom he has resided for the last thirty years, although himself a Pit River:

> "...and then Jesus Himself and his wife, her name was Mary, they went traveling all over the world but their little boy got sick and they had to come back to Lutuam Lake. This here Jesus he was a great doctor, he had lots of power, I guess he was the best gambler in the United States."

I could quote many other such expressions revealing the sacred character of gambling and the mystic nature of luck.

The other form of religious expression most nearly approaching a ritual among these people is in connection with shamanistic experience. Now this is the country of shamans par excellence. There are, at present, about a score of them, which is eight per cent of the tribe. You hear little else talked about except doctors and poisonings. But the most extraordinary part is the freedom with which they speak about it, provided of course that you are an Indian yourself or are being taken for one. We always think of poisoning by magic as a dark, shadowy and secret affair. And probably it is so at a later stage of culture, when the differentiation into white and black magic has already taken place.

That later stage is also the stage when *supercherie* and hoodwinking make their appearance. But here the belief is real and sincere, there can be no question of that. What more proof could be demanded than Sunset-Tracks, a shaman with whom I was living, *doctoring his own self?* He is an old blind man and he was knocked out of his buggy by an auto just as he started on a visit to his brother. He suffered many contusions but nevertheless got back into his buggy with the help of his wife, and they drove on to Hantiyu, a place twenty miles away. When he got there he was feeling pretty sick. That night his *poison* Raven came to see him. It must be explained here that by his "poison" a medicine-man means indifferently his power, his medicine, the poison actual or magical that he "shoots", the animal from which he derives it. It is all the same thing in Pit River psychology, and is expressed by the word *"damagomi"*.[1] On the other hand the poison calls the shaman *itu ai*, my father. So his poison Raven came to see him that night and told him that his shadow had been knocked out of him when he fell out of the buggy

> "and it stayed there on the ground while I went on to Hantiyu, and I guess I should have died if I stayed there, if Raven had not come to tell me. That's why I came back. Last night Bull Snake he put him back in my breath, he put my shadow back here in my breath. Bull Snake he is my poison too. He is pretty good poison, he is pretty strong fellow. Raven, he is my poison too. He always see everything. He live on top mountain there, on top Wadaqsudzi. Jim Lizard he is my poison too, but he is pretty mean fellow. He lie all the time. I can't trust him. Sometimes I am doctoring and he tell me that man he going to get all right and then make me ashamed because that man die. Sometime he quarrel

with my other poison. I hear him talking out there in the bush. Bull Snake he say: "What you think, Raven, you think our father he cure that man?" Then Jim Lizard he say: "Aw! let's go, that man going to die anyway, our father can't do nothing with him." Then Bull Frog he shake his finger at him, he say: "I am not asking *you*, I am asking this man here, I am asking Raven." Well, I am going to ask them tonight, if my *interpreter* comes tonight, Jack Steel he is always my interpreter, I have sent him word to come tonight, if he come I am going doctor myself."

"How can you doctor yourself?" I asked, "you can't suck yourself!"

"No, I can't suck myself. Maybe I get my brother Hantiyu Bill to come and do that. He is Indian doctor too. But tonight I just want to find out how long I am going to sick. Maybe I am going to be sick a month. Maybe I am going to be sick a long time. Maybe I am going to die. My poison he know. My poison he tell me."

The interpreter did come, and we held the "doctoring" that night. The old doctor got so excited when he heard his poisons coming near in answer to our calls that he danced almost into the fire, and yet his leg was so painfully swollen that he could not move it without groaning. He began to get well rapidly after this. The purpose of the interpreter, by the way, is to serve as a sort of link between the shaman and the world, not only the visible but the invisible world. All that the interpreter does is to repeat everything that the shaman says, but in a set intonation, and with a formalized ending. For instance, he calls in a loud voice to the poisons to assemble: "Come, Snake, come, Raven, come, Lizard, come, my poison!" Then he repeats the questions which the shaman puts to them. And it is also he who repeats their answers, which the shaman hears subjectively and repeats aloud in a more or less emoted and unintelligible fashion. For one thing the shaman speaks very fast then. But usually the interpreter is pretty well acquainted with his idiosyncrasies in garbling. However, he sometimes has to make him repeat. The exact value of the interpreter, in psychological terms, is not quite clear to me. My feeling is that the shaman is in a somewhat dangerous state of autism during the performance, a state into which he is in danger of sinking more and more, were it not for the precaution of anchoring his self in the outer world by means of the interpreter. Most shamans are markedly neurotic.

However, it must not be understood for a moment that their neurotic temperament is evidenced by the fact of their daily contact in terms of intimacy with their damagomis in the invisible world. For, the very same sort of intimacy marks the relation of any Indian who is not just "a plain common Indian" to his *dini-howi,*[2] his power, his protector, his luck, his medicine, or whatever may be the English word preferred by any individual Indian. Now, the dinihowi is absolutely the same thing as the damagomi except that the damagomi is more powerful and is only "for doctors". In other terms, there is somewhere in the woods some individual animal, some one particular deer, or a certain locust, or a certain weasel, some one individual denizen of the wilds with a particularly strong dose of life-power to his credit, and he is the fellow whose acquaintance you must make and whose friendship you must acquire, cultivate, and keep. Go into the woods and find him. Seek him in the lonely places, about the springs. Call to him. Go again. Starve yourself and go again. Call to him. Sing his song.

Try this song, try that song. Maybe he used to be somebody else's protector, somebody who died, and now he hears that song and he says: "That's my song, that's my brother's song,[3] it is a little bit different but it is almost like it, it must be somebody very much like my brother, I think I had better go and see." So he will come and take a look at you. He won't come very close because he is kind of wild. He has got to get used to you. But some day, perhaps after you have called him a long time and you feel lonely and you cry and you are all tired out and you fall asleep, that's because you feel him coming and you lose your senses, you are just like dead, then he comes and wakes you up. He will push your head and say: He! wake up! you sleep there long enough, go home now. That's all he will say but you know he is your dinihowi, he is your power, he is your medicine. Maybe he is good for hunting. Maybe he is good for gambling. You'll soon find out. You will see him again. You must come and call him again. You must not take him near people's houses. He might smell something bad there, some dead thing, some woman's blood, and then he will run away, and you can't catch him again. The more you chase him the wilder he gets. When you lose your power, you soon know it, your luck is gone, no use gambling, no use hunting, you may even lose your life.

I have unintentionally dropped into the manner of speech of my Pit River friends. What I have just said is not a quotation from any one man but a sort of composite picture of what I have heard from many. I do not want to go into the details of dinihowi hunting and visitation by damagomi. There are some exceedingly interesting psychological problems connected therewith, as well as with the details of shamanistic performances. It will form part of a detailed ethnographic study of this interesting tribe which I hope to be able to publish in the future. But I think I have said enough to give the feeling of the degree of intimacy and of daily intercourse with these animal protectors, these carriers of the life-power, these damagomis and dinihowis who by the way are not the animal in its generic or specific aspect, but just one certain individual of his species or of his genus. In other terms not Coyote, Deer or Weasel, but rather Mr. Weasel So-and-so, Mr. Deer So-and-so. Or, as one man said to me: "It's the same among the animals as among us, some of us have got power and luck, and others are just common Indians; some deer are just common deer, and others are doctors and chiefs among the deer; that's the ones you talk to."

No one animal is more especially sacred than any other. Silver Fox created the world with the help of Coyote. But neither of them is venerated in any way. There is not the least feeling of making these or any other animals into gods. I cannot insist too much upon that. In other places in California one gets the unmistakable feeling that Marumbda and Kuksu, or whatever their names in the local language, at any rate the Creator and his Counterpart are the lineal descendants of Coyote and Grey Fox. Here again I must forbear going into an exceedingly interesting subject of psychological significance.[4] The Pit River creation myth is one of the most interesting in the California series because it contains a most pure creation of *form* by means of intuitive thought. For Silver Fox made the world "by thinking": *haydutsila.* And every Pit River Indian knows two or three versions of it, and is interested in learning new ones, just as he is interested in learning new stories of the Coyote cycle, the Weasel cycle, or any of the million stories of that time, not so very long ago, when animals were men, or men were animals, whichever way you prefer to put it. For the matter of that, there is no real difference between men and animals from the point of view of the Pit River Indian. We must not forget that to him these stories are not historical narratives but literary dramas. They fascinate him because they embody in excellent artistic form the emotional and psychological problems of life, all this of course from the Indian point of view. You can always make a Pit River stop whatever he is doing and sit down, by telling a story, even when he knows it by heart. But he does not get any religious emotion out of it. His religious emotion he gets out of his intimate contact with the life-power that permeates the world.

This contact, this religious experience, is intimate, personal, individual. It is never cast into any prescribed form, much less into any ritual. All that development will come at a further stage in the evolution of the superorganic. But this most primitive stage is marked by extreme looseness and fortuitousness. No two men have the same dreams and one of the most commonly heard remarks about a shaman is: "I have never seen him doctor, I don't know how he works."

I hope I have given somewhat the feeling of the background of religious experience among these very primitive men. It is strongly alive even today and it is absolutely the only form of religion they have. Their conception of the mystical life-power is as decentralized and unorganized as their social organization. But neither in their doctorings, in their relations with damagomis or dinihowis, nor in their myths and tales is there anything which can even remotely be called God or a god.

The Gilak Monster and his Sister the Ceremonial Drum

It was Swan-woman who wove the first basket, the first
basket ever made.... she wanted something to keep her
ear-rings in, and her beads, and her comb.... so she thought
about making a basket, she thought about it, she thought
about weaving it

she went to see her sister... her sister was a woman who
knew a great deal about the mysterious things, about magic...
and now the Swan-woman asked her what she thought about it,
what she thought about this idea of hers of making a basket, of
making a basket by weaving

"yes, I think so... I think you can
do it.... altho it is a dangerous thing
to do.... something might happen while you
are doing it... there is danger in it... you

will have to be careful, you will have to be careful"

Swan-woman then went to see her friend Quail-woman.
Quail-woman also had magical force; her power was of
snakes... "...do you think it would be all right for

me to weave a basket?...do you think there
is too much danger in it...? I have been
thinking and thinking about it"

Quail-woman said nothing for a while. Then she said:
"yes, I think you can do it.... Go ahead, weave a
basket, but you will have to be careful.... As for
me, I will protect you against the dry ones, the
ones on land, but I have no power for water-things"

Swan-woman then commenced her basket,
and as she wove, she made a pattern: first,
a snake-pattern going all around; next she wove
a water-ripples pattern; and she added to it the
quail-crest-plume pattern (Quail-woman had given her
a feather from herself to keep among her weaving-materials).

So it was that Swan-woman made the first basket.

Then Quail-woman also made a basket for herself.
 The basket she made was a large basket, a very large basket;
it was this way: she wanted to give it to her husband for him
to give it to his people for them to store in it their crop
of acorns...... her husband was Hawk.

But after she commenced weaving it, she was sorry; she
hated giving it to her husband Hawk because he was running
with other women...

so she sat weaving and weaving, and feeling bad; she did
not want to give her basket....

At last she had finished the huge basket,
but she had made up her mind to run away

but everywhere she went, she left red tracks;

she went over rocky ground and she left red tracks

on the rocks; she crossed the creek and she left
red tracks on the rocks at the bottom; she thot:
"he will follow me, the Hawk my husband", and she
came back discouraged.

Now she took the large basket
to the creek to wash it -- she was
thinking... then she climbed into it and
went floating downstream toward the lake

then she thot: "I wish my house to become a stone-house!....
I wish my children to fall asleep; then
when I get to where I am going, I will
send them a dream, and they will know
how to reach me" (she had left enuf food
to last them for four days, dried meat,
acorn-meal, and other kinds of food)

now she was sailing down the river -- she floated
like that all night -- she floated to the middle of
the lake -- monsters came up on all sides... but they
saw the designs on the basket, the patterns of
snake, and of water-ripples, and of quail-plume,
and they were entranced

as the basket drifted near the shore;
she did not know hwere to go "shall I go
south? shall I go north? shall I go east?

shall I go west?...." and hwile she was
wondering hwere to go,

the GILAK-monster came soaring
in the air looking for people
to steal, and he saw her, and he
swooped down, and flew off with her to
his home in the mountains.

He goes flying thru the air... you can hear him
from afar... kinikinkinkiNIKINIKINI.........when his brother
hears him he opens the flap over the smoke-hole...
when his sister hears him she wakes up... she was their
younger sister, she was the Ceremonial Drum

she wakes up;
she yawns and stretches
her limbs, showing her long, sharp
teeth...

kinikinikiNIKINKINI... the Gilak is coming thru
the air, holding a man in his claws, he has a boy in his
claws, he has a woman in his claws, anyone he can pick

up in the lower country he brings home to his sister,

the Ceremonial Drum in their village in the mountains;

he brings them home, when his elder brother hears him

he opens the flap over the smoke-hole, and the Gilak

drops the man, the boy, the woman thru the smoke-hole...

the Ceremonial Drum opens her legs and chews them up and

spews forth the bones ----- there was a heaped-up ring

of them all around the house.

And inside the door there were two bears crouching

along the passage-way, and there were two snakes coiled

along the passage

and the watch-man was BUMBLEfly; he stood on

the roof of the house, watching all around --- he

had only one eye (the Gilak got mad one day because

he found him asleep on his watch --- so he gouged out

one eye --- "and the next time I find you asleep I'll

take out your other eye!!")

and the Gilak's elder brother had only one leg,

because the Gilak got mad one day when his elder

brother had forgotten to set the trap at the

inside doorway ---- so he cut off his elder brother's
leg and he said: "next time you forget to set the
trap, I'll cut off your other leg!!!"

inside the inner doorway there was a trap set ---- somebody
might catch the bears and the snakes asleep, but when he
got to the inner doorway the trap caught him and flung
him against the center-post and broke his back

that's hwere the Gilak People lived in the mountains -- that's
where the Gilak took Hawk's wife that time hwen he swooped
down on
her as she floated in the lake in the large basket; but he did not
drop her thru the smoke-hole; he took her in at the door

he said to his brother: "take care of her for me"
and he flew out again to look for people in the valleys
to feed to his sister, the Ceremonial Drum

hwen HAWK got home and found his woman gone, he felt
bad ---

he was sorry.... he cried, he said: "I'll go and get her back!"

His grandfather Coyote said: "...you had better not go... you

had better stay away from those

Gilak people... they are bad people...

they'll kill you!... it's too bad,

and I feel sorry for you, but you had

better not go... those Gilaks are hard
people to beat

and you don't know how!"

but Hawk wud not listen....

he rolled himself back and forth on the

ground, and feathers grew on him;

now he was a hawk

then he laid his bow-and-arrows on the

ground and tried himself for a short flight;

he went up a little way, and flew back again,

and swooped down to pick up his bow-and-arrows

and up he flew again, up into the air, toward the mountains.

Hwen he arrived at the place of the Gilaks, he rolled himself

on the ground, and rubbed off his feathers, and now he was

Hawk again

then he crept to the door

then he shot the two bears

then he shot the two snakes

then he rushed in and the trap

caught him and flung him against

the center-post and broke his back

the elder Gilak picked him up and threw

him to their sister; the Ceremonial

Drum opened her legs and chewed him up and

spat forth the bones thru the smoke-hole

and right away his grandfather Coyote Old Man

knew it that Hawk was dead; the old man cried

and rolled over and laid his head into the fire,

but his other grandson Hawk pulled him out by the feet.

Now Coyote Old Man set about recovering the bones of his
grandson;

he wanted the bones of his grandson; he wanted warriors to go

with him; first he went to see the FLINT brothers; Coyote
Old Man

went tonnnno-no-no-nonono..... limping along the trail with his

stick and carrying his little buckskin sac hanging from his neck

he arrived at their haus; he went in; he sat down by the

fire without saying anything... then he opened his litl sac
and he commenced pulling out of it a string of beads, he
pulled it out, he pulls it out, he finished pulling out;
there was quite a pile of beads; then Coyote Old Man
cut the string, and he made a knot at each end, and he put
one of the ends back into the litl buckskin sac hanging from
his neck; now he pushes the pile of beads across to the
Flints,

"here, this is for you, I want you to come and
    help me recover the bones of my grandson"

"all right, Grandfather, we will help you, you can
    count on us, we will be there at your place to-morrow"

and then ton-no-no-nonono....... old man Coyote went along
the trail, limping and leaning on his stick, to the
house of the Blue-bird brothers

                            he sat in front of the fire
and he commenced pulling out a long string of beads from
the litl sac hanging at his neck, he pulled it out, he
pulls it out, he finished pulling out; then he cut the
string and he made a knot at each end, and he put one end

back into his little sac "I want you two to come and
help me recover the bones of my grandson; they say you are
good warriors, that's what I have heard" "Yes, grandfather,
we are fear-for-nothing men, we can fight, we will help
you, yes, Grandfather, you can count on us"

and then ton-nnn-nononono....... Old Man Coyote went along
the trail to the house of the Towhee Brownbirds... "they say
you are good gamblers... that's what I have heard... I want you
to help me" "yes Grandfather, yes Grandfather, we have power
for gambling, we shoot straight, we'll help you, we'll be
there at your place to-morrow morning, you can count on us"

in the morning, they all started, the six of them and
Coyote Old Man, making for the mountains

                                    and on the way
Coyote Old Man had said: "Boys,
if you shud find a bit of punkwood
lying around somewhere, bring it to me,
I want it for a purpose."

                        And Coyote Old Man had said also:
                        "Boys, if somewhere along the trail

            you shud find a slab of

            rock lying around, bring it to me,

            I need it for something"

        and now they had arrived at the place of the Gilaks,

            way back in the back of the mountains, and Coyote

    Old Man hid his men in the bush while he went around

    the house, picking up the bones of his grandson Hawk

    from among the pile of bones that littered the ground

then Coyote Old Man put the bones of his grandson

into the little sac hanging from his neck, and he

took out of the sac the punkwood and the slab of rock

        then he lit fire to the punkwood, he crept to the

        door, and blew the smoke down the passage-way; it

        blinded the bears and the snakes, and they all slipped

        by; and at the inner door-way Coyote Old Man threw

        in the slab of rock; the trap caught the rock and

        hurled it against the center-post.

When the smoke cleared up, Coyote and his men were sitting

against the wall, humming a gambling-song

the older Gilak was very much surprised, but he said nothing;
he brot some firewood, threw it on the fire, and sat down,
watching the others

very soon they heard the younger Gilak flying home over the
mountains......kinikinikiniKINIKINIKINI...... he flew in at
the smoke-hole... "How did they get in?!" he shouted. His
older brother answered: "I don't know... I don't understand it...
the house got full of smoke and hwen it cleared up here
they are!.... I don't know how they got in, but they act as
if they had come to gamble"

Coyote Old Man spoke: "Yes, we have come to gamble... that is,
if you are not afraid of us.... or maybe you haven't got any
beads..." and he pulled the string of beads out of the little
buckskin sac hanging from his neck, he commenced pulling, he
pulls it out, he pulled it out, then he cut the string, he
tied each end into a knot, and he shoved one end back into
the sac; the beads made a big pile in front of him

"That's a lot of money!" said the Gilaks, "but we can cap it"
and they brot out their beads; it was just enough to cap
the other pile

and the Gilak said: "you had better be good gamblers, because we shoot straight... and I want to warn you: we don't play like children, for fun; and we don't guess by shooting out just our hands; oh no!... we guess with the arrows from our bows!.... so if you are afraid it is still time for you to quit, and we will take all the beads"

but the others had already started the song, and Coyote had given the bones to the Flints to hide; they were singing and swaying together, and they sang

"ho tunghstung yawallaneee
waki waki yawallaneee"

The younger Gilak was stringing his bow; he tested the string and made it hum; then he took an arrow and straightened it carefully... the others were singing and swaying; they were singing all together; they were singing fine

now the Gilak nocks the arrow, he draws it to the head, he shoots once, he shoots again; one arrow hit the elder Flint sideways and glanced off, one

arrow hit the younger Flint square and split in two
against his face

    Coyote Old Man said: "Good guessing! good
    shooting!! you hit us both times.... Now it's
    our turn to shoot" and he threw the bones
    across the fire to the Gilak

now the Gilaks take the bones and start their song

but the younger Gilak wud not stay still, he was jumping
sideways, fast, fast, now he is flying, darting from side to
side of the house, below the roof where it was dark, like an
angry wasp, buzzing the song

Coyote Old Man whispered to the Bluebirds: "you two do the
                       guessing!... shoot him next to the big toe,
                     that's where he keeps his heart!"

    now one Bluebird strings his bow while his brother
    shoots his medicine like a searchlight where it
    picks out the Gilak where he flies zig-zag in the
    darkness under the roof of the house

the arrow flies

and the Gilak fell down dead

the Brown Towhee Birds were dragging his

corpse toward the Ceremonial Drum -- she

was opening her legs... the elder Gilak

cried: "Don't do that!... She is his sister!!"

but they shot him too and threw both corpses to

the Ceremonial Drum -- she chewed them up and

spewed forth the bones thru the smoke-hole

now one Towhee said: "Brother, sing a song, and I will

stamp on the Drum to test if it's

a good sounding one"

they were stomping and dancing on the
Drum.... "It

booms fine!... Boom, boom, boom, boom... that's a

good drum!!..." they stomped so hard they

broke the drum

now they all were going to tear down

the house, but Bumble-Fly said: "No, give

it to me to live in, I haven't any place

to go, and it's a good house"

now Coyote Old Man told them to step outside for a

while, and leave him alone inside the house..... then he took

the bones of his grandson out of the buckskin sac hanging

from his neck; he tied the bones together into a bundle -- then

he tied the bundle with a string to his own ear and he lay

down to sleep by the side of the fire

soon his ear twitched;

Coyote sat up and looked around,

but there was no one in the house;

he lay down to sleep, again

and again his ear twitched -- Coyote sat up,

he sits up and looks around: there was no one

in the house

a third time his ear twitched

the fourth time a man was standing there

"Who are you?" said Coyote

"I am Hawk, your grandson!"

then Coyote Old Man called
to the others outside to come in

"Who is this man?"

"Why!!... that's Hawk, your grandson"

now they all started on their way back home, taking along
Hawk Chief and Quail-woman, and their children

when they were but a little distance from the village,
the people came out to meet them

then it was that Meadowlark cried: "What is that they are
bringing back with them??!!...
stinks like carrion!..." and he
screwed up his nose

Hawk was ashamed -- he called his brother aside --
he said: "they say I stink... I am ashamed... I'll go away!"
His brother said: "I'll go with you"

when Coyote Old Man missed his grandsons he cried; he
grabbed his walking-stick and hurried after them,
limping along the trail, following their tracks

when they had reached a fork in the trail where the trail
split in two directions, one Hawk said to his brother:
"you go that way... and I'll go this way"

When Coyote arrived at the fork in the trail he did not
know which way to go... first he ran one way for a short distance
then he stopped: "my other grandson will think I liked
his brother the best..." then he ran back to the fork and
started up that trail and ran a little way and stopped
"my other grandson will think I liked his brother best..."
and he ran back to the fork...... he was running back and
forth......

> then he stopped; he threw his cane high up in
> the air... it came down again and struck him
> on the head and cleaved him in twain

> the two halves of Coyote looked at each other: "You
> are I and I am you... now we can both go after my
> grandsons"

The Fury of Loon Woman

ONE MORNING, YEARS AGO, Loon Woman and Antelope sat together in winter camp and talked. After a while Loon took the baby Quail in her arms, and began to croon a lullaby song to her:

sol	stimu			dini hoo		
fa		dzuk			wi	hoo
mi						
re			ittu	llcg		
do		uy	dzi		ga dini	

sol	wi		stimu		
fa			dzuk		
mi					
re	gudzigu	lleg		ittu	lleg
do		dzi		uy	dzi

sol	dini hoo				
fa		wi	hoo	wi	
mi					
re				gudzigu	lleg
do		ga dini			dzi

"That's a nice song", Antelope said. "My mother used to sing it to me, but I never understood the words. Do you know what they mean?"

"Yes", said the Loon. "They are in the northern language. That song belongs to the Wolf People... 'stimudzukuy ittu dz-illeg'... dream for my child... 'dinihoowiga dinihoowigudzigu'... that he will have power."

"But that's singing", Antelope said.

"No, that's not singing", Loon replied. "That's the way they speak in the north country."

"Is that where you come from, Dr. Loon?" Antelope asked.

"Yes and No. I am a little like your Doctor Coyote here.... I belong everywhere.... I am a wanderer.... Wandering is a lonely life.... People don't like us Loons very much. It has something to do with a great-great-great-great-grandmother of ours. When she was very young she became disappointed, and in her fury she destroyed the world... you would hear that story if you go up north, I'm sure."

That evening, when everyone was sitting around the camp fire, Antelope said to Loon, "Doctor Loon, why don't you tell us the story about your great-great-great-great-grandmother who became disappointed and in her fury destroyed the world."

"All right", said Loon.

They were all living at Tulukuupi in a big winter house. It was Coyote's house. He had four boys and two girls. The boys were Wah the Bear, Tsimmu the Wolf, Ne tssale the Wildcat, and Yas the Weasel. The two girls were Lawiidza the Eagle and Qamawisla the Loon.

That winter there was another Old Man staying at Coyote's house. He was Aponaha the Cocoon Man, and with him was his son Makah-Awammiiyeewa the Pitch Eater... that's what they called him... the Pitch Eater. Makah-Awammiiyeewa was a fat white woodworm who lived under the bark of pine trees, sugar pine trees, up in the north country.

Every day the boys went out hunting while the old men, Coyote and Cocoon Man, sat on two stools at the back of the house rolling string and swapping stories. Cocoon Man wouldn't let his son go out with the boys. The fat woodworm was all white and clean, and his father didn't want him to get dirty.

One morning, after the boys had gone out hunting, the two girls sat by the fire weaving baskets. Lawiidza the Eagle Girl was quiet. She kept weaving her basket, and didn't speak much. But Qamawisla the Loon was a restless one. She kept going up and down the center-post ladder all the time. She would stand on the roof, and look around, and dance and sing. And when the boys came home that evening she teased them. The boys ate their supper and made their beds in the house. The girls went to their hut, outside, for the night.

The next morning, at dawn, Loon said to Eagle Girl: "Sister, I had a bad dream during the night. I dreamt that someone came and stole my beads."

Eagle Girl didn't say anything.

Then Loon looked into her skirt and cried: "My beads *are* gone! My beads *are* gone! So it wasn't a dream. Someone really came and stole my beads while I was asleep!"

"Why do you show your beads to the boys in the first place", Eagle Girl said. "I never show *my* beads!"

Loon was furious. She stormed back to the winter house where the boys had just sat down for breakfast. She went up on the roof. She looked down the smoke-hole and sang: "I want a man... I want a man... I want a man."

The boys didn't pay any attention to her.

So Loon sang again, louder: "I want a man... I want a man... I want a man!"

The boys kept on eating their mush.

Loon straddled the smoke-hole and let out the lightning: KLKTSHKLTSHIK... TSHLIK... TSHLIK.

The boys jumped up. "Hey! What's the matter with you. Are you crazy? You'll burn down the house!"

But Loon kept on singing: "I want a man... I want a man... I want a man." And she let out the lightning once again. KLKTSHKLTLTSHIK... TSHLIK... TSHLIK.

"Stop it! Stop it!" the boys cried. "You'll burn down the house!"

"I want a man... I want a man", Loon sang.

Bear went to the foot of the ladder. "OK. OK. Do you want me?"

"Go back. Go back. I want a man."

Wolf went to the foot of the ladder. "Do you want me?"

"Go back. Go back. I want a man."

Wildcat went to the foot of the ladder. "Do you want me?"

"Go back. Go back. I want a man."

Weasel went to the foot of the ladder. "Do you want me?"

"Go back. Go back. I want a man."

Finally Loon ran down the ladder into the house and grabbed the buckskin bundle from behind Cocoon Man's stool. "Here is the man I want", she said.

"Well you can't have him", Cocoon Man cried. "That's my son!"

But Loon dragged the bundle towards the center of the house. Cocoon Man dragged it back. Back and forth. The boys were laughing, egging them on.

"Let her have him. Let her have him", Weasel cried. "Otherwise she'll burn down the house. Let her have him. He's useless anyhow."

Old Man Coyote sat in the back of the house, silently rolling string.

In the confusion the bundle came unwrapped. And there he stood, the Woodworm, white and fat, blinking in the light, holding his little dagger.

The boys roared with laughter. "Look at him and his little dagger. Give him yours, Brother, to help him out."

Bear broke off a piece of his own spear, and they spliced it with the Woodworm's. Then Wolf. Then Wildcat. Even Weasel.

Now Woodworm had a great big spear. He tripped on it, and nearly fell down; but Loon caught him by the hand and dragged him to the center-post ladder.

Loon went up first, Woodworm behind her. The boys stood there, jeering at him. But Coyote got up. He took pity on his daughter. He sneaked up behind the center-post ladder. As

Woodworm was going up he snatched the spear away from him and threw it in the fire. Nobody saw him do it.

Loon was hurrying along, but Woodworm was lagging behind.

"Hurry up. Hurry up. Look! A storm is coming. Let's take refuge in that forest of junipers over yonder", she cried.

By the power of her thought Loon created a storm in the sky. Then she made a hut for them and a bed of tule reeds. Woodworm laid down on his face and spread his arms and legs. She tried to turn him over, but he wouldn't budge. Toward dawn she fell asleep exhausted.

Woodworm saw his chance. He got up and sneaked out into the forest. After searching around for a while he found an old burnt-out stump with a snag. He dragged it back to the hut and shoved it into her while she lay there snoring. Then he ran. He ran down through the rocky flats. He ran all the way to the rim rocks. He ran down to the winter house at Tulukuupi.

When the boys saw him return they became uneasy. "Where is your woman?" Bear asked. Woodworm didn't answer. Then they smelled the smoke and heard the rumbling far away.

"A fire is coming!" Weasel cried from the roof. "The whole world is burning! I hear Loon's laughter. We will all be destroyed!"

"Stop it, all of you!" Coyote Old Man got up from his stool in the back of the house.

"You, Wildcat, go get our brothers, the Spiders. They will make us a rope. You, Wolf, go find Wa Wa Lunneg... the One-Who-Has-Lost-All-His-Children... he's a powerful bow-man.

We'll tie a rope to one of his arrows and then we can all take refuge in the sky. Now move!"

So they went and fetched Wa Wa Lunneg, the Terrible Lizard, and the two spiders, Taha the Big Spider and Ne Neegha the Little Spider. When they returned everyone went right to work. Taha quickly hauled out his rope and tied it to one of Wa Wa Lunneg's arrows. Wa Wa Lunnneg took a firm stand under the smoke-hole. He leaned back... way... way... back. He pulled the bow string as far as it would go. Then he released the arrow. It went up... up... way up. It almost reached the sky. But the rope wasn't long enough and the arrow fell back into the house. Ne Neegha quickly hauled out his rope and spliced it to the end of his brother's. Lizard shot again. This time it reached the sky.

They were climbing up the rope, up and up toward the sky. Down below the winter house was burning, and Loon was stomping around furiously in the flames. She looked up and saw them. Cocoon Man. Woodworm. Bear. Eagle Girl. Weasel. Wolf. Wildcat. The Lizard. The Spiders. Old Man Coyote, her father, he was the last one in line. They were near the sky.

"My father... my father... ittu ai!" Loon cried.

"My daughter... oh my daughter... ittu wattawi... ittu wattawi!" Coyote Man moaned.

"Don't look down... keep your eyes shut... tsekuwi diimadanmi kindze'pa'qaswadzi", the others cried.

"Ittu ai! Ittu ai!"

"Ittu wattawi! Ittu wattawi!"

"Tsekuwi diimadanmi! Kindze'pa'qaswadzi!"

"Oh my father!" Coyote looked down. The rope broke. They all fell into the fire.

The timbers of the winter house were burning fiercely. Loon ran to her father and pulled him out of the flames. Then she found a flat winnowing basket and waited for the hearts to pop out.

One heart popped out. Pop. She caught it in her winnowing basket. She waited. Another heart popped out. Pop. She caught it in her winnowing basket.

She had caught all the hearts but one. It was the Lizard's heart. She waited. At last it popped out, very loud... POP. She held out her basket but the heart popped right through the basket... it zoomed right through the air... ZOOOM... and landed on top of Mt. Shasta. "That one will be my ruin!" Loon cried.

Loon took the hearts and made them into a necklace. For the rest of the day, and late into the night, she danced and sang around the smoking embers. When she had finished Loon walked back into the forest and found Old Man Coyote.

"Father", she said, "I know what I've done. I've spoiled the world. I've spoiled the world and other people are coming. Now I will be Loon, and you will be Coyote. We can never be together again. I will live in the lake, and you will live in the brush. But every morning at dawn, and every evening at dusk, I will cry from the lake. Then you will come to the edge of the brush, and you will answer me. That way you know I am living. And I will know you are still living too. Now I must go. You also, you go."

Doctor Loon had finished the tale. And now she sat silently gazing into the fire. Everyone was silent for a long, long while. Finally Grizzly spoke: "That isn't all there is to that story, Doctor Loon. There is another part. I heard it once before."

"Yes", said Loon. "There is a second part. But I don't feel like telling it tonight. Whenever I hear that story it makes me sad. Maybe I'll tell you the rest tomorrow - if I'm still here."

"Oh Doctor Loon!" the children exclaimed. "You can't go yet!"

"Please stay another day", Antelope added.

"All right", said Loon.

Then Old Man Coyote said good night to all the people, to the redwood trees, and the grass people, and the people of the night. Then they all went to sleep.

The next morning Fox Boy got up before everybody else and began to prepare the breakfast fire. He found a piece of hardwood in Father Bear's buckskin sack. Then he took a piece of punkwood, shaved off one end, then ground it into a small pile of fine powder. He placed the powder in a gouged-out hole in Father Bear's piece of hardwood. Then he found another small stick of wood, and he rested one end of the stick in the gouged-out hole. Placing the other end of the stick in the palm of his hand, he began to twirl and twirl the stick. But the fire wouldn't start. Fox rested for a moment, then he started all over again. No fire. He started again. Still no fire. Fox became furious. He began to curse the wood and stamp his feet.

Antelope had been watching him. "That's no way to make a fire", she said smiling. "Watch me."

She took the stick and twirled on it fast, fast, fast. The punk-wood began to smoke. She blew on it gently... gently. The wood began to flame.

"How do you do that, mother?" Fox asked. "Why doesn't it work for me?"

"You're not patient enough", she laughed.

Old Man Coyote stirred in his bed. "What's that sound? What's that sound? Is it raining? It sounds like water in the creek."

"Go back to sleep, Uncle", Fox said. "It's just mother... laughing."

That evening Loon continued the sad story of the Fury of Loon Woman.

Many years later Bluejay and his wife Tule Bird were living at the foot of Mt. Shasta. Bluejay was a good hunter, but for some time now he hadn't had much luck.

"I think there has been trouble around here", he said to his wife. "All the people are dead. I think Loon Woman did it! Her mother did the same thing once before."

The next morning Bluejay went out hunting in the direction of Mt. Shasta. He went hunting around. Then he heard the song. It was a very beautiful song. Bluejay searched and searched, but he couldn't find where it came from. He went back again the next morning. Once again he heard the song but he couldn't find where it came from. That evening he said to his wife: "Tomorrow I'll go to the top of the mountain if I have to!"

"You had better leave it alone", she replied.

The next morning Bluejay followed the song to the very tip of Mt. Shasta. The song was coming from underneath a little mound of earth. Bluejay scraped some of the earth away. The song came out more clearly. He scraped some more earth away, carefully. Then he found him. It was Lizard's heart... Wa Wa Lunneg... the One-Who-Had-Lost-All-His-Children... just a little bit of a thing ... singing in the earth. Bluejay wrapped the heart in some moss, put him in his quiver, and returned down the mountain to his wife. When Tule Bird saw the little heart she wept with pity. She put him in a basket of water, and then she laid him by the side of the fire to keep warm during the night.

In the morning it was a tiny baby. So they nursed him along. He grew bigger and bigger every day. Now he was a little boy. Bluejay made him a bow and some arrows. The little boy went around shooting at everything in sight. He loved to shoot his arrows straight up to the sky.

After a while a small bump began to grow on the little boy's forehead. The bump grew, and grew, and grew. One day, while hunting, the little boy shot the bump off his forehead. He picked it up and brought it home to his foster mother.

Tule Bird placed the bump in a small basket near the fire. Then the same thing happened. In the morning when they awoke they found another little boy. So they nursed him along. The two boys grew up like brothers. In time they both became great hunters.

Years later Bluejay and Tule Bird were sitting around winter-camp talking about the two young boys.

"It all has something to do with the Old Woman who burned the world", Bluejay said.

"What do you mean?" Tule Bird replied.

"I don't know. You have relatives who live on the lake near the Old Woman's house. Why not ask them?"

So the next day Tule Bird went to visit her relatives who lived by the lake.

"Yes. Old Woman Loon has something to do with it", they said. "At least we think so. She spends most of her time out in the middle of the lake. We've seen her out there, but we never go near. We're too afraid."

Tule Bird returned home. When she arrived back at the camp, she told her husband what the people had said.

The next morning Bluejay said to his youngest son, the little forehead boy: "Go and tell Old Woman Loon that you want to borrow her boat. Tell her that you want to fish and that you will pay her half your catch. While you are fishing watch the water carefully. There is something strange in there."

Late that evening Forehead Boy came running back to camp. "Father! Father!" he cried. "I saw it. It swims under the water and wears a necklace made of hearts. It came out of the water once and went into the Old Woman's house. I followed it there. The Old Woman was combing its hair. But there was a noise so I darted back into the water. It looked like a very beautiful little girl."

"Go back to the lake", Bluejay said the next morning. "But this time take my bow and arrows. If you see it again, take good aim. Don't miss."

Around noon Forehead Boy arrived at the Old Woman's house. "Loon", he said, "you are too old to fish. Lend me your boat. I am young and a very good fisherman. I will give you half my catch."

"All right", Loon said. "But don't stay out so long this time."

Forehead Boy rowed out to the middle of the lake. He kept his eyes on the water. Suddenly he saw something swimming by. It was a very beautiful little girl wearing a necklace made of hearts. Forehead Boy shot her, then he pulled the body into the boat and went right on fishing. He shot a lot of ducks and piled them on top of her body. Then he went back to shore.

"I got a lot of ducks", he said to the Old Woman. "But now I'm very tired and very hungry."

"Then go into the house and eat", Loon replied. "I've cooked supper for you."

Loon began to unload the ducks. Forehead Boy saw his chance and ran out the back door. He left his voice behind, singing the Lizard song.

Loon was still unloading the ducks. At last she smelt the blood. She threw the ducks out of the boat faster, faster. Then she found the body of her little girl.

"WOOOOOWOWOWOOW!" Loon gave out a long drawn out terrible cry.

The Forehead Boy was running now as fast as he could towards home. He heard Loon give out the lightning. The whole forest caught fire. But Bluejay was watching. With his thought he made a strong wind arise, and the wind blew out the fire. But Old Loon kept coming. She had almost caught Forehead Boy when his older brother, Wa Wa Lunneg, rose up from behind a bush where he had been hiding and shot the Old Loon dead.

The next morning Loon was getting ready to depart on her wanderings again. But before she went Old Man Coyote rummaged into his little buckskin sack and brought out a large, beautiful bead of pink magnesite and gave it to her.

"Oh thank you... thank you, Doctor Coyote", Loon said. "But you didn't have to do that."

Then Loon said goodbye to everyone. She gave an especially long hug to Oriole Girl for whom she had begun to feel a great attachment. Then she walked quietly to the stream and waded in. Suddenly, just like that, she was out of sight.

Fox Boy was mystified. He ran over to the stream and gazed into the pool of water. Then he came back to camp and said: "That beats me! That pool is very shallow over there... you can even see the pebbles on the bottom... but she was nowhere in sight. How could she get away?"

"Look!" Oriole Girl cried. "She left her doctor's cane. She must have forgotten it."

Antelope smiled.

"Maybe she left it for you to find, child."

"Well then why didn't she just give it to me?" Oriole Girl asked.

"Doctors do things like that, sometimes."

The Lariat

I. Fray Luis Comes West to Worst the Devil

Who was Fray Luis?

We do not really know. He had come from Old Spain, so much is clear. He may perhaps have been that second son of the Don Aniceto mentioned in a family record of the parish of Haro, and whose name was so curiously omitted by the scribe's oversight. The record reads:

> ...The second son of Don Aniceto after a turbulent youth was touched by the grace of God and entered holy orders. He took the habit of San Francis, and was sent to the Americas, to the missions of Alta California. Recognizing his indomitable energy, his superiors turned the adventurous spirit of the man to the greater glory of God, and thus it was that he travelled from one Mission to another along the Coast of the Pacific Ocean, entering the wild hills covered with forests to preach the Holy Doctrine to the savage Indians of the woods. Until the Devil, Father of all Malice, alarmed at his success, counselled their priests to kill him, and he was crowned with the glory of the martyrs. The third son of Don Aniceto, Don Jaime, studied in Salamanca....

But even if his name had not been so strangely omitted, we would still remain in doubt as to his identity, for like many friars of that time he was known only by his nom de religion: Fray Luis. Fray Luis he remains for us, may God rest his passionate soul!

o ◑ o

Fray Luis came to Monterey in California, in the days of the Indians. He came to save their pagan souls, but as we shall see, he used the powers of sorcery, once, and lost his own. We may find some excuse for his sin in the violence of the passion of a man surrendered to God, in his agony as the day drew near when he would be forced to witness the profanation, the rape of his own soul. For, was not that Indian girl part and parcel of his soul? He himself had redeemed her. He himself had instructed her in the true faith. He himself had poured the waters of baptism over her lovely head.... The water had trickled down her throat, and a drop ran between her breasts. They were full and goat-shaped, like most Indians', and he associated them vaguely in his mind with the aroma of chocolate scented with vanilla.

And now he must perform another sacrament, bind her to the object of her carnal desire, a handsome half-breed, a half-savage, a youth in whose eyes lurked the gleam of untamed passions. He must deliver his dove into such claws. It would have been better indeed to leave her a pagan.... To find one's soul revealed only to be forced to prostitute it, and in the very name of God's sacred ministry!

Let us be charitable and realize the enormous temptation for such a mind in its agony to clutch at a straw and turn for help to the very monsters he had come to destroy. The monsters helped him. They gave him their power. He used it. Then, in the terror of his repentance, he betrayed his new masters, he went back to his own God. But the monsters had hold of him by a rope. The monsters had hold of one end, and the other end was girt around his loins. An unbreakable rope, a vaquero's reata, a monk's cord....

Struggle, struggle, Fray Luis! The monsters are pulling, pulling, dragging you down.... Ah! It is useless, Fray Luis. You gave them your soul. Down you go.

◦ ◑ ◦

Who was Fray Luis?

Who he was appears best from his own curious diary:

...Wednesday, Feast of San Fernando, Confessor and Martyr. I arrived here last night, at this Mission of San Carlos Borromeo del Carmelo, and very tired. Fray Bernardo is Superior of this Mission which is a very thriving one having been the pet of Fray Junipero, may his soul rest in Heaven. And it surely must, for he earned it, as does any one who comes here from the South by following the Coast. A more villainous country I have never seen. There are neither roads nor trails. I would have done better to come roundabout by the Valley and Mission Soledad, but I tried to take a short cut and came directly along the Coast through the country of those wild Esselen Indians whom I hope so much to convert. But it was an infernal trip and my donkey agrees with me. I shall not be able to ride him for a week. And yet I walked a great deal of the time during the last four days, so much so that I wore out a new pair of sandals and the bottom of my cassock is in shreds. Usually during my journeys into the rough country I wrap it around my waist, it is so much easier to walk or ride, and I don't think that our father San Francis was dreaming of American Missions, we do enough penance in this wilderness, but this time it was worse penance yet, lacerating my bare legs with the thorns of the trail. I must either wrap my legs with strips of buckskin like some of these Indians or wear leather trousers like the vaqueros. That will shock that old maid of Fray Bernardo and he will send a long epistle to Mexico. Fussy old mollycoddle, trotting from one warehouse to another, he prays the mass of Saint Tallow, Saint Wool and Saint Corn. May he be granted as many days of indulgence as all the heads of cattle he has made the converts raise for the Church. That is enough in any case to send him straight to heaven, for the old eunuch knows not temptation and his only sins are those of old women - grumbling and avariciousness. Well, each one serves God according to his own talent, I tame wild horses and he makes them work. I wear out my sandals and tear my cassock and risk an arrow in the seat thereof or a more vital spot to bring the effulgent light of the true faith to these lost sheep sunk in the dark labyrinth of superstitious slavery. "Come, my brothers, the life is not in your trees and in your rocks, it is in Our Father, He who made us and all, the only God. See Him behind the tree, under the rock, all beauty, incandescent and terrible, lovely in the image of His Son. Come and adore the true God." But evidently I should amend it thus: "Come and work for Fray Bernardo of the Tallow." Fray Tallow! I will wrap my cassock around my waist, if I please, and wear boots and spurs, beautiful silver spurs, and a wide sombrero to save my tonsure from the sun, I'll tie a bright silk around my neck, I'll mount a wild stallion, I'll turn in the saddle and thumb my nose at you, I'll ride to the hills.... Father in Heaven, Jesus, Saint Fernando, Angel of my guard, come and save me! Chase this devil away! Scourge me, beat me! Oh, my God, why must thou always tempt me? Have pity! Has it not been enough?...

∘ ◍ ∘

Fray Luis must have spent a night of remorse, for the next day he writes in a more chastened mood:

I spent the morning with Fray Bernardo, making the rounds of the Mission. We had to visit everything, the tallow works, the piles of hides, the granaries, the tile works and the adoberia. The good padre is very proud of it all, of the good order, of the prosperousness, of the apparent contentment of the Indians. They are working in their usual lazy way, and they smiled when we passed. Their eyes followed Fray Bernardo and I could see that they were fond of him. Well, he gives them plenty of atole, and he does not whip them much. This noon I tasted the pozole myself, and I found a lot of meat scraps in it, much more than we ever put in at San Antonio or at San Juan Capistrano or any of the other missions where I have stayed. No wonder the Indians here are so fat. And I didn't notice any of the sullen looks of San Antonio, nothing but that shadow of gentle sadness over their eyes. They all have it, these Indians, when they are away from their rancherias. Fray Bernardo talked and talked in his tight Catalonian accent. I think he comes from Mallorca or another one of the Balearic Islands. Anyway he is the most active old man I ever saw. Quite an administrator and very pious. But oh! so garrulous and such a child in some ways. For instance, he took me this afternoon to see the magnificent beach which is not far from the Mission. Well, there, just on the other side of the rocks, there was an Indian girl bathing and all naked. What a scolding she got from Fray Tallow! "...Didn't that hussy know that it was strictly against the rules? She would get the lash for that! Shameless wench, why didn't she go back among the gentiles?..." all of this in mixed Rumsen and Catalan. The poor little one was standing, before us, with tears in her eyes, very much distressed at all the violence, but quite plainly not understanding a word of what he said. I questioned her in the language of Mission San Antonio where she came from. She said she belonged to a rancheria of Esselenes, back in the hills near the Coast between here and San Antonio, that she had only been here a week, that she did not understand the language of the Rumsen Indians, nor the language of the white men, why was this man so angry, was he a powerful sorcerer, and would I please ask him not to give her the evil eye. When I interpreted all this, Fray Bernardo tore his hair. "What? Another language yet? Misericordious Father in Heaven, how many languages are there in this California? I have been here all these years and I never heard of Helens before. And now who is going to instruct this poor wild girl?" I assured him that I would, since I knew the Sextapay language and this girl seemed to understand it. At this he was very much relieved, and we went home, he to his account-books and I to my worries. I am worried. I think that innocently I put an evil thought into that girl's heart. I need not have explained to her the cause of Brother Tallow's wrath. I should have invented some excuse. But my wits were asleep because I was struggling with the work of translation. At first she didn't understand. She looked at me incredulously. Then she seemed to comprehend, and she began to laugh, but she suddenly checked herself, and slowly the blush of shame crept all over her dark skin. And I who had been innocent of any thought up to this moment, felt myself blushing by contagion. Seeing this, the girl turned and fled toward the rocks where she had left her zarape.

At supper we had a visitor, a young vaquero, the son of a settler who lives way down the Coast. He was one of the leather-jacket soldiers in the first expedition with Captain Portola, and he deserted with several others who could not endure the arrogance and harshness of Lieutenant Fagés. Later they were amnestied, but this man had already taken a wife in the tribe where he took refuge, precisely the Esselen tribe of today's naked girl. He had already a son of two years when the news of the amnesty reached him in the rancheria of gentiles where he was living, with another deserter. His companion returned, but he chose to stay. Now he has a house down the Coast. He is getting old. His son, who was telling us all this story at supper, is a typical vaquero, tall and handsome, with the Indian blood in him showing only in his eyes and hair, and perhaps his temper, for after some courteous conversation he suddenly dropped into a sullen mood and became silent. Fray Bernardo says that he had never heard him speak so long before. It appears that he has been a frequent visitor at the Mission of late. Fray Bernardo likes him and encourages him to come for he thinks that he may perhaps use him to take care of the Mission cattle. There is a rule here imposed by the Military Authorities forbidding to let any Indian ride horseback. They seem to think that all the converts and neophytes would run away if they had a chance, but I say that it is no use to tie them here unless they are truly willing to stay in the service of the true God, and why not cut off their legs while we are at it! Tomorrow I intend to celebrate the Mass for the soul of that one who died seven years ago tomorrow through my fault. *Ay, Dios de mis pecados!*

II. And Finds Him Entrenched in the Wilderness

On top of a ridge facing the Pacific Ocean, at dawn.

Silence everywhere, except for the confused murmur of the sea, three thousand feet below. The steep slopes facing the Occident are still in darkness. Here and there small bands of deer are grazing, moving about like shadows.

The sun rises, peeking over the top of the furthest ridge on the orient. A wild country is revealed, a maze of ridges and canyons filled with fog. The silence is broken. The birds twitter everywhere. The blue jays greet one another.

BLUEJAY: "Good morning, Sir. How did you spend the night?"

ANOTHER BLUEJAY: "Very well, thank you. What a fine morning, isn't it? But I am afraid the day is going to be hot."

FIRST BLUEJAY: "I think that you are right. I like the hot weather, myself, but my wife suffers very much."

SECOND BLUEJAY: "Well, I am like you. I can stand any kind of weather, myself. It's all the same to me. But it's pretty hard on the little ones. My family is just beginning to fly."

FIRST BLUEJAY: "So is mine. And let me tell you, between us, I'll be glad when they are out on their own for good. All this worry...!"

SECOND BLUEJAY: "Yes, yes, a family is a great responsibility, a great responsibility.... Say! Do look at that Magpie, will you?... Went by with her nose in the air and not even a good morning for civility! The hussy!"

FIRST BLUEJAY: "Oh, don't pay any attention to such people.... Excuse me a minute, I see a worm.... Here, have a bit of worm with me.... Don't mention it, nothing at all. And by the way, have you heard about a white man passing through here the other day?"

SECOND BLUEJAY: "Yes, I did. I didn't see him myself, but I have been told about it. First white man here in years and years, they say... except for that old fellow who has been living here ever since my grandfather was a little boy."

FIRST BLUEJAY: "Oh, he doesn't count! He is just like our Indian people. He is just like them... and his son even more so. But white men are different. At least that's what they say. They say you can't understand white people. They say you never can tell what they are going to do, that's what they say. About this white man, they tell me he went by here at nearly sundown, and that he split himself in two, once."

SECOND BLUEJAY: "What d'you mean, split himself in two? I didn't hear about that."

FIRST BLUEJAY: "Yes, split himself in two... that's what they tell me, and one half looked like a doe, with long ears, but it had a tail like a puma, and the other half had only two legs and no tail, like a wildcat, and the white man's head went with that. But I don't believe it, do you?"

SECOND BLUEJAY: "You can't tell! Don't you remember how we all got excited when our white man, that old fellow, came here? He did the same thing, and now you don't even think it's strange."

FIRST BLUEJAY: "Yes, that's quite true. Well, I wonder what it all means. My grandfather says there must be something wrong about so many white men coming into this country. But you know how old folks are! They don't like anything new. Now, these two here, this old man and his son, they have been here for a long time, and yet they have never done us any harm."

A BIG BUCK who has been scratching his hide against the bark of a pine-tree: "They don't do me and my people as much harm as our own Indians!"

A LITTLE FOX: "Oh, I would love to see a white man, a real white man."

An Old Fox: "Keep quiet, you little fool! You don't know what you are talking about! You are just like that old brainless buck. He ought to know better! My friends, let me tell you, I used to live way up north from here, where there is a river emptying into the sea. Then lots of white men came there, not just two, but many of them. And I saw the white men kill so many of my relatives that I moved down here. They use a special kind of bow and arrows. It makes Pum! and you have no time to dodge. If they ever come here it will be our end! But I don't think they will ever come so far...."

The Two Bluejays: "Tschak! tschak! tschak! Run everybody, all of you! I see two Indians coming this way along the ridge!"

The deer leap down the slope, crashing through the brush. The foxes slink away. Silence again. Way down below, the ocean is sparkling and stretches away, away to the end of the sky. A maze of ridges and hillsides covered with chaparral, already beginning to dance in the heat of early morning.

Halfway down the slope, a little flat, with a few Indian huts, and a small house of logs and adobe, with a chimney. Smoke rises from the chimney. Below, a condor is soaring around and around. The sun shines on his back and wings at times. Hundreds of feet below him, near the water, sea gulls are specks of white gainst the blue.

Not a sail on the Ocean. Silence. Silence. Immensity. Every little while, a puff of breeze brings the faint din of the roar of the breakers.

∘ ◯ ∘

"Father, there is a new friar, at the Mission."

"Ah.... Give me another piece of meat, boy. That's tender meat! Your cousin brought it yesterday. He takes good care of me while you are away.... He said he saw some cattle below the Spring of the Madronyo. You had better ride there this morning. They'll be drifting into the back hills soon, and get wild again."

"All right. I'll go.... This monk is tall and lean. He does not speak like Fray Bernardo. He speaks more like you."

"Maybe he comes from Castilla.... You had better take the sorrel colt. He needs a ride."

"You mean I need to be bucked off?" the young man laughed. His teeth were white. His skin was very dark. He tore into another piece of venison. Then he spoke again, his mouth full:

"I don't like his manners. He is polite enough... but he is not friendly, like Fray Bernardo."

"Lots of people are like that, son, in my country. It does not signify. It's just their manner....I think it's going to rain soon.... And your cousin says that a bear killed another cow."

"Bear, fiddlesticks! A bear with bow and arrows, yes! Probably one of his own relatives!"

"*Bueno, que importa?* If they are his relatives, then they are yours also. They have always brought me a share of their hunt, all these years. Let them take a beef once in a while!"

"Yes, but they take too many!"

"No, no, my son, it's the bears."

"Oh, you and your bears! ...I wish the bears would leave us alone and go to the Mission and eat that new friar!"

"Tsch! you mustn't speak that way about a holy friar!"

The young man scowled. "Well I don't like that holy friar. He looks more like a holy demon to me, with his burning eyes and his long nose. His nose is too long, and besides it is crooked!"

"But what matters the shape of his nose? If he were a horse, I would say yes. But a priest is different."

"No, he is just like a horse, your holy friar. He looks like a horse who has never been well broken. I'll bet that before long he will buck old Fray Bernardo and his corrals to hell!"

"Oh, be silent! Don't bother me with your Mission and your friars! What do I care?... Go and saddle your horse! I hope he does buck you off to punish you for your impiety. Some day God will punish you! Go and saddle your horse!... I'll clean here!"

"*Bueno, bueno,* I am going. Don't get angry. But just one thing more.... That old Indian who is *major-domo* at the Mission, you know whom I mean, old Saturnino...."

But this time the old man interrupted him with a volley of oaths. He was livid with anger.

"I have already forbidden you time and again to speak to me about him! I don't know who he is, and I don't want to know! If you ever do it again...." But the young vaquero was already flying toward the corrals.

∘ ◖ ∘

Old Esteban Berenda, who flew into such a rage at the mere mention of Saturnino's name, was one of the leather-jacket soldiers who had come with Captain Portolá on his first expedition of discovery. He was one of the deserters who preferred taking their chance in the wilderness rather than endure the famous Lieutenant Fagés.

And now old Esteban was hardly a white man any longer. When the Indians had found him wandering half-starved and in rags through the canyons, they took pity on him. They fed him. He built a house for himself and that Indian girl he had taken for his wife. He built it of logs and adobe on the little flat overlooking the ocean. There was a spring there. It had been the site of an Indian village, or rancheria, for countless generations.

When the news of the pardon of the deserters had reached him, years before, and he had first dared show himself in the open, he obtained a few cattle and a mare and her foal from the Mission. He tended them carefully. He begged the Indians not to shoot them, and for a long time the bears were afraid of these new creatures. His herd grew. His little boy grew. He taught him to ride on the old gentle mare. He taught him to throw the reata, a little one at first, on the small calves. It was a hard life and lonely. The boy spoke Spanish with him and Esselen with his mother. His name was Ruiz, but the Indians called him Kinikilali, "Who-is-that?" That was his Indian name. Very soon he was taming colts and lassoing big bulls. He grew up more like an Indian boy than a white man. But after his mother died and he spent most of the time riding with his father, the Spaniard appeared in him, in an odd mixture. And now old Esteban sat for days with his back against the house and Ruiz-Kinikilali rode after the cattle. They roamed everywhere on the hillsides. He did not know how many there were. They roamed on the other side of the ridge into the tangled country and got wild. The Indians shot those when they could. That was all right. The bears or the mountain lions would get them anyhow. The young vaquero rode the ridge constantly, looking for wanderers, trying to drive them back toward the ocean slopes. But it was hard work driving alone. He was secretly teaching Pawi-maliay-hapa "Many Arrows" to ride horseback. Pawi was his cousin and his chum. But Ruiz did not tell his father anything about it. It was strictly forbidden to let any gentile Indian ride, and Esteban was an old soldier with a profound respect for orders. Besides he did not want any excuse for the military to come down there and shake him out of his dream. He had been asleep now for ten years, gone back wild, sucked back into the wild country, surrounded by the devils who lived in the air, under the rocks and in the old trees. The Indians arranged matters with these devils and he did not have to bother about them. He felt safe and contented in his solitude, and free to dream away for hours about nothing. He did not want anybody to come and disturb him, priest or soldier.

So, Ruiz did not tell his father that Pawi was learning to ride. Ruiz felt that something must be done. It was all very well for the old man to say that he didn't care, and what was the use of so many cattle anyway? At the rate they were going they would have none left in a few years. The bears were getting more and more bold and numerous. Esteban would not hunt them any more. He said it was too dangerous, and besides how could he be sure but that some day they might make a mistake and lasso a bear who was really a sorcerer in disguise? Maybe there was no such thing as that, in the midst of the *gente de razon,* in the neighborhood of towns and churches with the Holy Sacrament to watch over the country, and he himself was a *cristiano rancio* and believed only in the God of his ancestors, but he knew also that medicine-men could change themselves into bears. This was a wild country and it was true here even though it were not true somewhere else.

This hunting of bears was a dangerous business. When Esteban settled there, and the bears began to kill his cows, he decided that he must either get rid of them or lose all his little herd. But of course he had no rifle, and he had never learned to use a bow and arrows even to kill small game. His wife's people had always given him a share of their hunt. But to kill a bear with a bow and arrow takes a very good hunter, and a very brave one, because a merely wounded bear is mightily dangerous. So Esteban thought of a stratagem. He could lasso the bear, and this would give time for his companions to shoot several arrows at short range. It was an exceedingly risky sort of hunting, because a bear, unlike a horse or a bull, instead of choking on the reata, will grab it and pull. If he does not get an arrow through the heart very soon, there is nothing for it but to let go of the reata and get away as quickly as possible. Esteban lost many good reatas in this way. This was serious, because a reata takes the best part of a raw-hide and about three days' work in cutting the long strands and braiding. Not only he lost reatas, but twice he lost his horse: once when the reata *turns* got too tight around the horn of the saddle and he had to jump off to save himself, and once when the horse stumbled and fell, luckily he was thrown headlong and clear of the animal. Moreover, the hunt had to take place at night, by moonlight, since it is impossible to get near enough to a bear in the daytime. So Esteban and his helpers would hide in the bushes at night near a cow freshly killed by a bear and wait for him to come back to the carcass for another meal. Esteban had a good horse, a "caballo de reata", that is, a horse at once quick and obedient, a horse that could jump ten feet from a standstill on the merest tap of a spur and yet not dance a fandango after ten minutes of hard work cutting herd, "arrebatar", as they call it. Ruiz had a horse not quite so good, too nervous. As soon as he heard the bear coming crackling through the brush and smelled the pungent, disquieting smell, he would begin to snort. And Ruiz himself, in the first years when he began to hunt with his father, sitting there on his horse in the dark, with the reata unslung and the loop all ready, waiting there in the shadow, peering into the moonlit space and trying to rehearse all the turns and twists, when he heard the crackling and snapping in the chaparral, coming, and stopping, and coming again, and stopping, and coming again, his spurs went ting-a-ling-ling, he just couldn't help it though he heard his father cursing him in his beard and the Indians sniggering.

Ruiz was left-handed with the reata, and that helped a great deal because between both of them they could stretch the bear nicely. Then the Indians would fill him with arrows, almost point blank. The whole thing was done quickly, silently, in the space of an Ave Maria after Esteban shouted "Ahora" and the two horses dashed out into the moonlight. Then the Indians would stamp a short dance of expiation around the dead bear, going three times around one way, then back the other way round once, and calling him "Elder Brother, Chief, now you are happy!"

The old man would coil his reata and go home. Ruiz-Kinikilali used to lag behind, coiling and re-coiling his reata, watching the dance, feeling queer and upset. And one day he just naturally took his place in the row of stamping men, but he never told his father this.

And now Esteban Berenda was getting old and did not hunt bears any more. He sat in the sun in front of his house and watched the sea. Maybe the Philippine galleon would appear soon on its way south. He sat in the sun and blinked at the sea. He was thinking of his dead wife, the Indian woman. She had been fat and silent. He sat in the sun, blinking, looking at a pueblo of whitewashed houses shimmering in the haze. He didn't hunt any more. He didn't even ride after the cattle any more. Let Ruiz attend to that. He was young. Let the bears kill a few cows. It did not matter. Plenty of cattle yet, grazing on the sunny hillsides. Let the Indians shoot a few on the other side of the ridge. It did not matter. They were his own people, or his wife's, or his son's anyway. Ruiz, they called him Kinikilali. Which was the better name? He sat in front of his house, blinking in the sun, on the little flat, and the ocean stretching away blue and sparkling.

His wife had been dead now for more than ten years. He had wanted to bury her, but her relatives insisted on burning her body. He usually let them have their way. It was so far to the Mission, a full day's ride on a good horse. He hardly ever went there, and as for the Presidio, he shunned it altogether. If they wanted to burn her body, let them do it. After all, she belonged to them. He himself would always remain a good *cristiano,* but the Mission was so far, and he had lived all alone here for so long, he did not know what to think any more, and perhaps their ways were the best ways for this kind of country. After all, it was their country and they knew her, they knew her spirits, all kinds of people who lived in the air or inside the trees, some of them were birds or animals. The padres called them devils. Perhaps they were devils. Esteban did not know. He was not versed in theology. He himself had never seen a devil, and the Indians had always been good to him. He liked them, but, for all the years he had lived among them he had never gotten to know them. He had never even gotten to know his wife. He had loved her very deeply, and after she died he always felt lonely.

Esteban was old and he sat on a stump with his back to the house, looking at the ocean. He sat for hours looking at the ocean. He sat looking at the ocean, dreaming.

Sometimes a ship hove in sight, way out at sea, a galleon from the Philippines, homeward bound with her cargo. Such ships headed straight for Cape Mendocino and then sailed south along the coast, bound for the ports of Lower California and the coast of Sinaloa. Their sight excited him strangely.

The old man sat on his stump, looking at the ocean, dreaming. He would never go home now. He thought of the sun baked plains of La Mancha and a pueblo of white houses shimmering in the haze.

Why didn't he saddle his horse and look at the cattle? Oh! What did he care about cattle now! Let his boy do the riding. He was young.

∘ ◐ ∘

It is a strange country, that wild Coast of the Esselen Indians, where Esteban had taken refuge, a strange country, beckoning from afar. Curiously enough it is almost impossible to get there. And yet it is not a case of burning deserts or impassable snows. The country lies smiling under a pleasant sky, with water in every brook and long grass on the hillside. True enough, it is everywhere exceedingly steep, and the canyons wind in very tortuous fashion, so that the whole country is a labyrinth without any natural avenues. This may account partly for the unsettled state of the region even at the present day. But there must be something else. There must be some reason why every time you try to get into that country you find yourself balked and finally turning back after much fatigue. Why does that place keep itself so remote, as if holding a secret, brooding under the sun? It lies at the edge of the water, rising like a wall, gazing moodily over the same ocean, towards China and the other side of the world. And back of the wall there are the deep canyons, and the tall pine and the hillsides of brush in the mysterious glare of noontime. What does it mean? How can a thing be so wild that is so full of life and charming variety, of young trees and deer grazing in the gay clearings, of the chatter of bluejays, and the red trunks of the madronyos. And yet it is so wild in there that you cry with the loneliness of it. You feel a creeping panic in your heart. Perhaps it is because we are civilized and do not understand those things. We have other gods, and we can no longer pray to the tree.

At any rate this is the place where Fray Luis wished to proselyte. He knew that the Esselen lived in there. They were "gentiles," unconverted Indians. They never came to the Missions. They were utterly pagan. Fray Luis burned with desire to convert them. He kept thinking about it.

He had found it impossible to reach the Esselen from San Antonio, but he thought he might perhaps succeed from Carmel. And that is why when he caine to that Mission he decided to go directly by the coast line. Nobody else but Fray Luis would have been foolhardy enough to try it. But he succeeded and managed to come through, as we have seen in his diary. On that trip he saw no Indian rancherias. Several times he saw small parties of Indians at a distance, but although he called to them and made friendly signs they always vanished from sight. And yet he had the feeling that he was constantly watched. A queer sensation to go through those wild lonely woods and feel all the time that someone is watching you. You can imagine the deer scattering at the approach of his mule. In his diary he calls it a donkey but it was probably a mule. The son of Don Aniceto would have called a mule a donkey. And in the distance, parties of brown men, stark naked as were the Indians of those days, with the bow in the left hand, the arrows under the right armpit. They would not stop when he called them.

How is it that Fray Luis had missed the little flat with the house of Esteban on that memorable journey from San Antonio Mission, when he had pushed and dragged his mule for three days through the wilderness? He could have seen it easily from the place where the trail from the beach crosses the ridge, a trail made by generations of Indians. It climbs like a staircase from the rocky shore more than three thousand feet below, up, up, steeper and steeper, over the face of the limestone cliff, hot like a furnace. It emerges on the summit of the ridge and then plunges down on the other side, down into the canyada where another Indian village stood on a sheltered flat. Here there were more of the conical huts, and also a ceremonial house with its smoke-hole door on the roof. This other village, deep in the canyon, was hidden from the ridge, but the little flat on the ocean slope could easily be seen. Yet Fray Luis missed it.

Perhaps he was looking the other way, or perhaps it was in the late afternoon when he passed, that strange time when the spirit of anguish is abroad, leading fear by the hand, and he was looking for a good camping place, hurrying, oppressed. That time in the late afternoon, when the sun is low over the water and the deer come out of the canyadas to graze on the little flats and on the hillsides. Go there some day and sit down with your back against a tree. Keep quiet, do not move, keep very quiet. Just sit there, still as a stone.

Do you hear what the jays are saying over your head, up there in the branches? Bluejay is saying: "Hey! who is that there? Are you asleep or dead? Dead man, I guess, went to sleep there and died. That's all right, Mr. Squirrel, walk right over him, don't be afraid, come right up. Some nice pine cones on this tree, up there at the top. Just getting ripe and the nuts still juicy and fresh. Only don't drop the scales right over me! My gracious, haven't you got any manners? Come right up, Mr. Deer, come right up this way, and nobody in sight, fine grass for Mrs. Deer and the little Fawn, fat little fawn, how old is he? Say ... just look at that Woodpecker, will you? Did you ever see anybody so busy? Peck, peck, peck, woodpecker, now go get another nut. Fine for Mrs. Bluejay, Chief Bluejay, that's my name. Hard winter, plenty nuts and acorns in little holes, thank you, Mr. Chief Woodpecker, because I am sure you are a chief also.... Sh! look out there everybody! I hear someone coming along the trail.... I hear a horse's footfalls.... I hear the jingling of spurs.... Quick, Deer, run, run!"

A vaquero passes along the trail, slouching in the saddle.

BLUEJAY: "That's right! You own the world, don't you.... Well, you can come back now, Mr. Deer. He's gone. Why! look who is here, Chief Weasel himself and Mr. Coyote."

COYOTE: "You mean Mr. Chief Coyote, don't you? Chief Coyote, Doctor Coyote, that's me. Everybody knows me. I am the one. I am a chief, I am a medicine-man. I am a runner, I can run fast, I know all kinds of running songs, I made the world, at least I made half of it, the worst half, that's the best half...."

BLUEJAY: "Well, then, why didn't you make a woman for yourself, even half of one? Where is your wife, eh?"

COYOTE: "Hey! Hey! I have no wife. I have no wife. I must go look for a wife. I can't stop here talking with you. I must go look for a wife."

WEASEL: "I see some people coming up the trail from below."

BLUEJAY: "Yes, I have been watching them, too. Just Indians ... with a load of abalones and mussels. How slow they are going. Must be a heavy load. That's all right, Mr. Deer, plenty of time, plenty of time."

Three men and a woman appear on the ridge. The men are entirely naked. The woman wears a grass skirt. They all carry pack-baskets on their backs, slung from the forehead. The woman's is smaller and slung from a strap across the chest, just above the breasts. They bulge from under it. They are all panting heavily. They squat on their hams, to ease their packs on the ground. They say nothing.

BLUEJAY: "That's right, take a rest, boys ... and girl. Nice girl, that, just right for Coyote, but maybe not big enough! Ha! Ha! Long climb up here, boys, and quite a way to the rancheria, yet. And how was the fishing? Well, you might answer something, you dummiesl Aw, they don't know anything. Not a one of them is a medicine-man. Just common Indians. That's right, get up and on your way, you have got quite a bit of trail, yet, even if it is downhill, and the sun is getting pretty low ...."

WEASEL: "Who were they? I don't know any of them."

BLUEJAY: "Oh, some fellows from the rancheria down there. I have seen them before. Just common people, nobody in particular. Ho-hum.... I am getting sleepy. Sun is almost in the water. I feel all tired out . . . working too hard . . . I don't know what you people would do without me. Well, goodnight, Father Sun, I think your brother is coming out pretty soon. Here, move away, you, that's my twig...."

WEASEL: "I have a brother in that rancheria. A fine young Indian. Pawi-maliay-hapa, that's his name. Fine young fellow. Good hunter. He always calls me when he is going on a hunt. He has got my song and I lead him to the game. I go ahead and I wait for him. I sit on a rock and wait for him to catch up. I lead him to the game. I like that young fellow. He knows my song. He always remembers to call me."

A Cricket: "I know somebody in that rancheria too. He is my father. An old blind man. He is a doctor. He knows lots of songs. He knows songs for everything."

A puma comes along the trail, in the moonlight.

Puma: "I know the one you mean. He is my father, too, that old blind man. He knows my song. I heard him calling a while ago, down there, but I am not going right now. I am hungry. I am going to hunt tonight. A nice fat deer for me."

He stretches himself lazily. He looks at the moon rising over the Ventanas and lets out a long, querying roar. It makes a beetle jump.

The Beetle: "Great Scott, man! Couldn't you give us a warning? Look how you woke that little owl."

The Owl: "No, I wasn't asleep. I was just thinking... I was thinking about these new people, these white people... I wonder who they are...."

The Beetle: "Well, Sir, I'll tell you what I know, which is what I heard a grandfather of mine tell me when I was a little boy. He used to tell me about some people on the other side of the water. Very powerful people, he said, and very wise. They knew a great many things, more than these Indians. That's what I heard my grandfather tell. And I have figured it out from the way he said they lived, that these new white men are the same people... except that they are foolish, that's what I don't understand, unless it is that they have forgotten what they used to know. Or maybe their heart got all dried up inside of them...."

A **Pine Tree**: "You are an old man, Beetle, and you talk too much. I am older than you and yet...."

A **Redwood**: "Whenever the wind blows the pine trees have to talk."

The Ventana Cone to the Santa Lucia Peak: "You look all grey, old man, in the moonlight."

Santa Lucia Peak: "Shut up!"

An Indian's voice rises in the night, a young voice, singing: "Hey-hey-hey-ho-he-hey... my heart is crying... where is my power?... hey-hey-hey-ho... you have taken my power away... tumas! iyo! come, my spirits, come, my power... she left me because I am ugly and crooked... she left me... hey-hey-hey... my heart is crying...."

The Night Wind: "I am cold and dry. I am lonely."

III. The Devil Sets a Trap

Meanwhile, at the Mission of the Carmel, Fray Luis was catechizing his especial neophyte, that girl who had run away from the Esselen tribe. He had other neophytes also to instruct, men and women from the Rumsen tribe, mostly people from the Carmel Valley and from the rancherias along the lower part of the Salinas River, but he was especially interested in the Esselen girl because she was the only Esselen at the Mission. It was the first time that anyone from that wild tribe had been persuaded to leave the mountains and come to the Mission. In fact she had come of her own free will. She had appeared there, one morning, foot-sore and hungry, and very shy, just a few days before Fray

Luis arrived. She was of course a godsend for that friar whose very ambition was precisely to bring the light of the true God to the wild Esselens. And so he spent more of his time learning the Esselen language from her than teaching her the catechism.

He wrote in that curious diary of his: "Dia de St. Gertrudis, Virgin, and a most beautiful day, too, with an amethyst tint spread over the valley. I called this to the attention of Fray Bernardo. 'Yes, yes,' quoth he, 'very beautiful, very beautiful, and just think, my dear Fray Luis, just think of how much grain could be raised here and exported if only the home Government were not so short-sighted in its policy!'... and he went on to explain a lot of things which I did not understand. That Catalan has a head on his shoulders! I also asked my little wild beauty what they call that color in her language. She said there was no name for it, but it made her think of the inside of an abalone shell. I asked why. 'Because it isn't real', she answered. She says things like that, all the time, that make me restless. And then when I try to teach her the catechism I find her so stupid. Strange little animal! But anyway she is a good teacher when it comes to language. Only, what a devil of a language! You say everything upside down. It reminds me more of the Sextapay of San Antonio than of the Rumsen of these parts. As soon as I know enough of it I am going down into that country. I am burning to convert these poor wild Esselenes. Something is drawing me to that place. I have been dreaming of it, several times, curious dreams, almost nightmares. I must go there. I did not come here to get fat and lazy. As soon as I know enough of the language I will go. God will help me... and if He has reserved me for the fate of the martyrs, blessed be His will, say I. What more do I crave than to expiate my sins? What could be sweeter than to forget?... I must make a friend of that young vaquero. He may be able to help me. They say that his father and he are the only white men living down there, and that they are on good terms with the Indians. The young fellow was here again last night. I must say I don't like him, and I don't know why. There is something subtly insolent in his bearing. It's not his manners. He is boorish enough, but so is everybody in this country. For the matter of that, he is not half as boorish as the people of the Presidio, the Commander of the garrison included, and they have not the excuse of having been raised like an animal of the wilds.... Fray Luis! remember that you are no longer in Salamanca, this cassock is not a capa, remember above all that this crucifix is not the hilt of your sword. Ah! my sword, my lovely, my pretty, where are you? Is it a sin to remember you, and your lithe body, my mistress, my very myself? Is it a sin? Is it not enough to stand with patience and humility this fellow's searching gaze? And how well he rides! I believe that is what I am jealous of. What a figure he would make in the streets of Sevilla!... Bah! This is an edifying diary I keep. Shame on you, Fray Luis, pray, Fray Luis, you unworthy monk, take your breviary and pray, I'll discipline you, I'll make you forget, I'll scourge you, the lash for you, the lash for the devil in you...

....I don't know how many strokes I gave my poor back, enough anyway to bring the blood... but I feel better, I will sleep peacefully tonight. Saint Gertrude, you noble virgin, I offer my pain to you. I offer it for this poor Indian girl, take her under your protection.... Nine o'clock! To bed, to bed, three hours only before Matins and the shaking hand of Fray Tallow on my shoulder. How I do hate to hear his Catalan rasp from under my dreams, 'Come, come, Fray Luis, up with you, it's almost a quarter past midnight. Come, come, to the chapel, don't be so lazy'... well, to bed!"

Look at these two men at Matins, in the echoing empty church, just these two, on either side of the nave, each one with a candle to his book, throwing back and forth the versicle and the response, the two voices alternating in sonorous cadence, monotonously for an hour, while outside the constellations swing around the pole toward the chilly dawn. Ah! the wonderful technique in all ritual, this losing of one's own self into the magma of a cosmic rhythm, the dissolving of the individual and his pain, and his sorrow, and all that effort to hold the self together. To stamp a chant around a drum under the moon, or to sing a psalm in the gloom of the nave, two techniques for two cultures, but the same psychological problem, at bottom, and after all very much the same treatment.... Therein lies the beauty of prayer in common. And therefore it was a wise monastic rule that held these two friars to what may seem an almost meaningless, an unnecessary formality. Two monks holding Matins by themselves, just exactly as if they had been a whole congregation. It makes one think of those white men who live alone in the tropics, and dress every evening for supper. Two monks, two white monks, isolated in their Mission, on the outskirts of a not even very civilized colony, and surrounded by more than two hundred so-called "converts", and several thousand not far outside the Mission abode walls, in all the rancherias, practising actively all the rites of magic and sorcery, these two white monks they had need, indeed, to hold on tight to all the forms and formalities of their own culture... one of these two especially.

∘ ◯ ∘

At the Carmel Mission old Saturnino was the mayor-domo. That is to say, he was a combination of sacristan and Indian chief. The tribe under his care were the Indians corralled inside the Mission adobe walls. He bullied them, especially the neophytes. Very few people remembered his Indian name. He was Saturnino, *el mayordomo,* and one of the oldest and first converts. He said he was a Rumsen, from one of the furthest villages up the valley. But the older Indians at the Mission smiled ironically at this. According to them that village up the valley had only been his hiding place for a while, a certain long time ago, when he had run away from the vengeance of his own Esselen tribe. He had relatives at that rancheria up the valley, and they hid him for a while. But he would not tell them what it was he had done. After a time they advised him to take refuge at the Mission which had then just been started. But all that was long ago, nobody remembered very much about it, and if old Saturnino caught you talking about it, or even suspected you were talking about it, down came your portion of pozole at the next meal. And it would be no use complaining to the padre, because the mayor-domo would simply say that he had heard you swearing, and the padre would believe him.

Saturnino had charge of the pozoleria, of the chapel, and of the "nunnery". It was he who saw to it that all the unmarried women were in there at nightfall before he locked the door, and then he turned the key over to Fray Bernardo. He enjoyed locking them up for the night. He also had charge of the routine catechization of the neophytes. He lined them up in the morning. They squatted on the ground. He squatted on a chair in front of them, with his feet on the edge of the seat. When a padre appeared in the offing he put his feet down. When the padre had disappeared the feet went up again. He sing-songed: "Our Father", and the Indians in front of him repeated, "our father". They knew that tolerably well. He sing-songed: "who are in heaven", they repeated something very close to it. He sing-songed: "may thy reign come." They mumbled something. He sing-songed: "may thy will." There was a feeble murmur. He sing-songed: "be done on earth as well as in heaven." Only one or two voices answered in a jumble of Rumsen words that sounded faintly like the Spanish. Saturnino would roll his eyes and click his tongue, and look significantly towards the pozoleria, and then he would fairly shout: "give us our daily bread." Everybody woke up and repeated: "Give us our daily bread." And so on, by lulls and storms for an hour. After which they went back to work with a sigh of relief.

And he went back to his reatas. They were his joy, his love, his consolation. He was a reata-maker. He kept his materials in the pozoleria, thongs of rawhide, long, very long strips, of an even width all the way for the forty or fifty feet of their length, cut as they had been from a single hide, round and round the edge. His tools, an old razor blade, a whetstone, a deer's antler for a marlinespike, and his teeth. He made reatas for the vaqueros of Monterey, and sold them. That was all his little benefice.

When a vaquero came to the Mission old Saturnino would ask: "And how is the reata?" as one might say: how is your baby? And sometimes they would bring him a reata for repair. If it was one of his own make, he would almost weep. He would cry: "But how did it happen? Don't tell me! You have been dragging firewood with it, or you staked your horse. Don't tell me no, don't tell me you broke it in the corral. My reatas don't break in the corral. My reatas will hold the biggest bull. Don't my reatas hold bears? Look at old Esteban, down the Coast to the south, he always tries to keep one of my reatas saved away for hunting bears. But that shameless son of his always steals them, and then he does just like you, he drags logs with it down the mountain. Don't tell me no. I know you did. Well, I will repair it this time, but this is the last time. All right, go and sin no more." This last remark said not at all as a joke but very seriously. He and Fray Bernardo had had several arguments about it. Saturnino could see no impiety in it. Fray Bernardo was totally lacking in the sense of humor.

◦ ◑ ◦

The afternoon was dragging lazily over the Mission.

The Mission was like a little town surrounded by a wall. Besides the church, there were the Indian quarters for the unmarried men, the Indian quarters for the girls (also called the nunnery), the pozoleria or kitchen where the mush was cooked in a great cauldron, the carpenter shop, various storerooms. One corner of the great courtyard was occupied by a crew of Indians making adobe bricks, and was known as the adoberia. Some were mixing the clay with the straw. Others were pouring the mixture in the molds. Rows of abodes in all stages of drying were arrayed on the ground. Even when everything else was silent in the Mission there was activity in the adoberia, and somebody was singing there. Sometimes a single voice, repeating over and over the same monotonous air. Sometimes a chorus, with a thud of stamping feet to mark the cadence. The padres knew that many of the songs were of a religious character, but they did not know which. On the other hand many of the songs were love songs, gambling songs, hunting songs, and the like.

It was wise to let the prisoners have some consolation. Most padres were men like Fray Bernardo, little given to speculation, content with sincere outward conformity. They got along fairly well with the Indians. They made them work, and were pretty severe at meting out punishment, at times. But they were not curious. They left the Indians alone as to their inner life. They did not ask questions. They were blissfully ignorant alike of all beliefs and customs of the unconverted or gentile living all over the country, and of all the gossip that went on inside the walls of the Mission. The adoberia was of course the clearing-house or exchange for all news. If a sorcerer caused the death of someone in a distant village, the fact was soon discussed and commented on in the adoberia. There were all kinds of intrigues and jealousies carried on. Some of the Indians were suspected by the others of "squealing" to the padres. Some of the Indians had really become sincerely habituated to their conversion. But most of them had been forcibly brought in by the dragoons, and baptized without their knowing it. Unbaptized neophytes were supposed to be still free to leave the Mission at their will, but converts belonged to the Mission and could not leave it.

Men like Fray Luis were rare. The Indians hated them. Fray Luis would never have made anybody work. He himself did not care whether he ate pozole or a juicy piece of venison. Material wealth was a very difficult thing for him to keep his mind on. Nor had he any sense of discipline. If he saw an Indian climbing over the wall he would never think of shouting an alarm, for the simple reason that the fact made no impression on his mind. But he was forever asking questions, forever thrusting his long nose into their private affairs. At any moment you might suddenly realize that he had been standing silently over you in plain sight, listening to your conversation, while you and a friend were heatedly discussing some tribal affair. And already he understood a lot of Rumsen. As for Esselen, that fool of a girl was teaching him. He wanted to know all about the Indian religion, as if that were any business for the white man. The few who were his especially reserved catechumens feared him even more. They longed for the days of Saturnino's classes. They dreaded this long thin torturer with the burning eyes and the long febrile hands shooting out of the brown sleeves. He was not content with "yes" and "no", he was not content with even a faultless repetition of prayers, he forced you to think and to know why this was so or so. He asked questions, he made you think, he made your head ache. He took possession of you and made you his slave. He was not even good-naturedly paternal like Fray Bernardo, with a kind of smile of approval and a pat on the head. His eyes burned and grew wide. He talked and talked. He made you feel like him. He made you see all sorts of things. Then he would leave you abruptly and walk off to his cell without a word, his long legs striding across the courtyard, and you felt chilly all of a sudden and looked up to see if there was a cloud. But no, the sun was beating down as usual. The crew was working in the adoberia. You knew they had been watching you, suspecting you. They would ask: "What does the old coyote want to know, now? What did you tell him? He is a sorcerer himself, watch out for him, don't tell him anything, he knows too much already!"

That was one of the peculiarities of Fray Luis. He would go straight across the courtyard, instead of following the arcades all around like any dignified person. Fray Bernardo once tried to remonstrate with him. Fray Bernardo was Father Superior after all. He first put the matter to him plainly, but Fray Luis did not seem to understand what he meant. So Fray Bernardo explained patiently that it was necessary to be dignified on account of the Indians. Fray Bernardo was rubbing his fat hands nervously. Fray Luis stood stooping over him, looking at him intently. Fray Bernardo began to perspire, and his face got red. He lost his presence of mind completely. He mumbled: "Well never mind, do as you like, it doesn't matter anyway", and proceeded right across the courtyard to his own cell. He was trotting as usual when he was agitated. Fray Luis went around the arcades with his own legs.... They arrived at the same moment at the doors of their cells, which were contiguous. Fray Luis waited for Fray Bernardo to pass and open his door. Then he passed by, and opened his own door. Fray Bernardo slammed his door shut. A few minutes later he could hear Fray Luis scourging himself. Fray Bernardo sighed: "What a saint! But he will drive me crazy!"

∘ ◯ ∘

The afternoon was dragging lazily over the Mission.

There was a lull in the adoberia. The boom of the breakers on the beach drifted over the wall. Gulls flew overhead on their way to the laguna. Old Saturnino was plaiting a reata in his corner. Sunlight filled the courtyard.

Fray Luis was instructing his Esselen girl. He sat on the ground of the arcade with his back against a column, his knees drawn up under his chin, his long hands grasping his ankles. The sun had moved and was beating down on him, but he did not seem to notice it. The girl kept retreating and retreating with the shade. She was getting sleepier and sleepier. But she opened her eyes more and more wide in listening. She liked his voice. She wished he would never stop. Once she went to sleep completely, and had a short dream. She woke up with a start. She winked several times. Then she laid her head against his knees. Then she began very, very gently to snore. When he heard the snore, Fray Luis stopped instantly, and his face went white. The interruption made the girl stop her breathing. She moved uneasily and her head almost rolled off Fray Luis' knees. His long hand shot out and pushed the head back on his knees. The girl's bosom resumed its regular heaving. Fray Luis was still pale with anger. He murmured: "Imbecile!" Then with great careful movements he reached for his rosary and commenced telling his beads. The sun now was reaching her body sprawled there, her face buried in the monk's robe. She was snoring quite loudly. Fray Bernardo trotted by. He stopped with a jerk. His jaw dropped. Then a wide smile spread over his face. He put his finger to his lips and with a large wink he tiptoed by. Fray Luis had not even seen him. He was telling his beads, looking at the seagulls circling overhead with shrill cries. Several Indians passed by, with wide grins on their faces. The adoberia was buzzing with suppressed laughter.

BANG! BANG! BANG! "E-e-e-e-i-ya-Hou!! Abren las puertas! No esten dormidos! Dispiertense, que aque viene la costa del Sur!" Wake up! Wake up and open the doors, for here comes the coast from the south!

Everybody jumped up. The doorman scrambled to his feet. The adoberos stopped drinking and gossiping, with broad smiles on their faces. The girl stopped snoring and woke up. Fray Luis snapped his rosary in anger. The knocking on the massive gates of the patio continued, and now a rollicking song in Spanish came from the other side, in a high tenor voice. Every verse was of four lines and the last line was in the Esselen language. All the Indians were roaring with laughter.

The great gates were opened. A vaquero dashed through, with his horse, in a whirlwind of dust. He pulled up halfway to the center, and all those in the adoberia could see him stick his spur in the under part of the belly back of the cincha. The horse started on a crazy round of bucking, twisting, sunfishing, backhopping, and every other sort of misbehavior. The Indians were roaring and yelling. Fray Bernardo came out of his cell, hurriedly buttoning his cassock, and winking in the strong sunlight.

When he saw him, Kinikilali stroked his horse's neck and made him quit. He jumped off and kissed Fray Bernardo's hand. Fray Bernardo made the sign of the Cross on the boy's forehead, then he raised him and embraced him.

"And where do you come from, now?"

"Well, Your Reverence sent for me and here I am. I started last night just before sundown, and I took a good sleep at the Little River, and then I came up, and here I am at your orders...."

"Bueno, bueno, chico, muy bien.... All the cattle are spread all over the place, everywhere, and we are losing them. All these boys from Monterey are no good. They are all right with the guitar, and some of them can throw the reata, but I can't depend on them. And anyway I can't have them around here with so many girls in the nunnery. I need you. You must bring in all the cattle that belong to the Mission. We will brand the calves."

"But, Father, how can I bring them in with me alone on a horse. You know I can't do it!"

"Sh! sh! sh! Some of them can ride... but everybody afoot as soon as you get down into the valley, you hear me?"

"All right, little grandfather. I'll send for my cousin. He is a good rider already... sh! sh!"

They both laughed.

"Father, I have to go to Monterey, tonight...."

"Go with God, my son."

Ruiz Berenda, or Kinikilali, kissed Fray Bernardo's hand. Then he turned and leaped in the saddle. He gave another yell, the doors opened, and he went out bucking in a swirl of dust. The massive gates creaked shut again.

The girl had slunk away long ago. Fray Luis was still sitting with his back against the pillar, telling his beads. The rays of the sun struck his face slantingly, with sudden patches of dark shadow on one side.

The late afternoon was descending on the Mission. The seagulls were returning overhead. It grew chilly. Fray Luis got up and strode across the courtyard to the Church.

IV. AND BAITS IT

Ruiz was riding along the Ridge, his gaze wandering over the chaparral, peering down into the woods, looking for straying cattle. He was riding along, lazily, sitting sideways in the saddle, but silent. He very seldom sang. He was riding along the Ridge on a hot afternoon. The saddle leathers creaked, the spurs made a jangling tinkle in cadence. The horse walked with a long-gaited stride.

The vaquero heard a whistle behind him, and stopped. He turned and saw Pawi hurrying after him along the trail. Pawi was his cousin on his mother's side. That is, Pawi's mother and his own mother had been sisters. So they called each other "elder brother", and "younger brother", in the Indian language. But they were nearly of the same age. Pawi was a good hunter. When he went out hunting, he observed all the rules. He abstained from any meat. He rubbed himself with bear grease. He called to the Four Masters of the Hunt, Puma, Bear, Eagle, Fish-Hawk. Then he called to whatever it was he was going to hunt: "Brother, you must let me kill you. My people are hungry. We need food. You must not run away and hide."Then he called to his own medicine, who was Weasel: "Come, my power, tumas iyo! Come Weasel, come my power, lead me to the game, lead me to the deer." Pawi-maliay-hapa was a good hunter.

Pawi was ordinarily a gay sort of fellow, rather reckless, ready for any kind of fun. He had high cheekbones and eyes that gave one a curious impression of being able to stretch lengthwise. His hair was very long, reaching almost to his waist. He usually wore it tightly wound in a knot. Then when he let it loose, it waved over his back like a stallion's mane.

But he looked worried that day, and full of concern, as he hurried after Ruiz. The vaquero had dismounted and sat on a log, holding his horse by a long horsehair rope. Pawi greeted him: "Hey! brother."

"Hey! brother", answered Ruiz, and he added, "Where were you?"

"Down there at the spring by the fallen madronyo. I saw you pass along the ridge and hurried after you. Listen! brother, there is a dead cow down there, by the spring. Something is wrong."

The vaquero sat still and said nothing for a long time. He was looking at the ocean. Pawi was squatting, idly toying with an arrow. He would curve it between his fingers, and then sight down the shaft to see if it was straight. Finally Ruiz-Kinikilali broke the silence, "It was a bear that killed her, wasn't it?" he asked.

"Yes."

Another long silence. Then the vaquero spoke: "That makes three since the month began!" There was bitterness and anger in his voice. He added, "I wish my father would wake up! Some day a bear will eat him, too, right where he sits dreaming all day. At this rate, there will be no cattle left before the rains. And just when we were getting a good herd! It seems a shame. Listen, Pawi, Pawi-maliay-hapa, we must do something!" Pawi did not answer, he kept on straightening arrows between his fingers. Ruiz spoke again. "I tell you we must kill that bear, you and I. This horse is good, now, under the reata. And you never had a better bow than this one."

Pawi smiled. "Yes, it is a good, strong bow. That was very springy sinew I backed it with. It was from the neck of that young horse who broke his leg, you remember? Do you know, Kinikilali, I think that horse sinew is better than deer. Let's kill all the horses, Kini, and make sinew. Then we will go to the white village and kill all the soldiers and the medicine men with the long skirts and make sinew of them too. Maybe they would make even better sinew than horses."

He was laughing. Now he stood up to test his bow, and show his chum how far he could shoot with the bow backed with horse sinew. With one end stuck in the ground, he bent the other end across his knee and strung it. Now he picked out an arrow, and straightened it. Now he knocked it, and he began the draw. He was standing with his feet close together, body slightly bent forward from the straight muscular thighs and a little to the left, as if about to fall, just posed over. He let fly, and kept his position for a second, the right hand drawn back almost to the cheek, his eyes following the flight of the arrow. It descended and stuck in the ground far away. Pawi turned back to his cousin with a smile of pride. Then he squatted again, and once more looked worried.

He looked at the ground for awhile, then looked at Ruiz full in the face, and said slowly, "I don't like it, little brother."

"Why not? You are not afraid, Pawi, I know you are not afraid."

"Yes, I am afraid, of course, I am afraid. You don't know who that bear is."

"Neither do you."

"No, I don't. But he may be somebody just the same. I don't like it, I tell you. Even suppose he is just a bear and not a person, it's too risky hunting him without your father's help. How are you going to keep him from grabbing the reata, if there is only one reata on him?"

"Oh don't worry about that. Anyway that's what you will be there for, to shoot him full of arrows before he gets to my end of the reata. And if he gets too close, well, I'll let go of the turns and all I lose is a good reata and a bearskin. Listen, brother, just think of all the bear grease you will get, all for yourself, nobody to divide with. Maybe you will get four hands of bead-strings in exchange at the Rumsen villages. It seems the bears are leaving their country... I wonder if that is why there are so many around here."

The two of them were silent for awhile. The afternoon was stretching towards evening. Pawi spoke again: "I will help you... but I don't like it, I tell you. I will help you, because I can't say no to you. You keep after me like that and I can't help myself, although I know it is not good. This morning I started out to hunt and I looked for my protector, that Weasel. Pretty soon I saw him ahead of me on the trail. He was leading me to the game, as usual, running on ahead and stopping on a rock or on top of a log, waiting for me to catch up. Then I got thirsty and I went to the spring of the Fallen Madronyo to get a drink. That is where I saw the dead cow. I was looking at the tracks of that bear and Weasel got angry. He did not want me to stop there, he did not want me to stay there. He kept jumping up and down, and scolding. He would run off and come back to scold and run off again. That's when I saw you. I wish now I had listened to him."

Ruiz laughed, "Leave your Weasel alone. What does Weasel know about hunting bears? He may be all right for game without hearts, like deer and rabbits, but he doesn't know anything about bears. Your weasel is a coward...."

"Hush, Kinikilali, you fool! He might hear you." And Pawi peered all around suspiciously. He was scared and angry. "What do you speak like that for? Are you trying to spoil my luck? What's the matter with you?" He was glaring at his cousin. Ruiz tried to pass it off as a joke. But Pawi was angry now.

"Kini, I wish you were all Indian, like us."

"I am Indian enough, big brother. I don't like the whites."

"Then why do you do the things you do?"

"What is it that I do? What are you scolding me for, now?"

"You know very well. I mean that woman."

"There you are! I knew you were going to come out with that, sooner or later. Well, what about it? Can I help it if the woman left her husband? I had nothing to do with it."

"Some people say that you did not, and again some people say that you did."

"No, I did not, Pawi. She left him because she was afraid of his medicine. She says that he had too much power and she was afraid of it. She says it was his power that killed their little child. It was too strong and it killed the child. She says he was not careful enough. He came into her camp right after curing sick people, and sometimes he still had his medicine hat with him, even with a new devil he had just caught, stuck right there in among the feathers. I don't blame her for leaving him."

"Yes, he is too careless, I know that. Young doctors are careless. But why do you have to get mixed up with it? Why did you take her down there, down to the white man's camp?"

"I did not take her down there, Pawi. She went there herself."

"But you go there all the time too. Our people have heard about it from the Rumsen. They say that you are making love to her."

"And what if I do! I have a right to. She has no husband."

"Yes she has a husband. Her people never paid back the marriage gifts. Hualala is still her husband, till the gifts are paid back."

"Well, his people have not paid back what she gave for him, either."

"They don't have to. It was she who left him."

"Yes, but it was his fault."

"Who says that? I have not heard the chiefs say that, and they are the ones to decide."

"What do the chiefs say, Pawi?" Ruiz was eager now.

"I don't know. They are not talking yet, but the people are grumbling. Some people are very angry with you. Some people say Hualala has a right to kill you now."

"I am not afraid of him!"

"You had better be! He is a powerful doctor, even if he is young. His medicine is strong and it will surely kill you if he sends it after you. His medicine will do it, I know, because he has a right to kill you, as far as I can see."

Ruiz-Kinikilali was beginning to be a little frightened for all his customary insouciance. He said plaintively, "Are you also against me, brother?"

"No, I am not against you, but what can I do? I can't protect you against his medicine. You ought to have some strong power to work against his. You ought to get some strong doctor to work for you. You are rich, you can hire a good doctor."

"What about the old blind man, Amomuths?"

Pawi laughed bitterly. "That's all you can think of!"

"Isn't he the most powerful doctor around here?"

"Sure he is! But he is the girl's grandfather, too!"

"No, he isn't! I know very well who he is. He is my mother's uncle."

"Let me see.... Yes, that's right, he is. Well, that only makes it worse for you and that girl, because you and she must be some kind of distant blood relations. I don't know what the old people will say about it. They are sure to know it. They always know what people are related. That's all they have to think about. But maybe they won't remember it if they don't want to. But if they want to, they will surely remember it. And that makes it worse for you. Why can't you leave women alone, Kini, little brother? Look at me, I have no troubles like that. I know very well that a man can't be a hunter, and fool with women at the same time, at least not let them get into his heart. My Weasel wouldn't like it. He would be jealous. And you, you who want to hunt bears, you make love to the wife of a sorcerer, granddaughter of another sorcerer, the most powerful one in the tribe, and your own blood relation. I tell you I wish you were all Indian. You wouldn't be such a fool, then. At least, why don't you offer to pay him back the marriage gifts?"

"Of course, I will!" cried Ruiz. "I will give him twice as much as he gave for her."

Pawi was silent for awhile. Then he said: "Maybe he will take it, and maybe he won't. I don't know. He is a strange fellow, that young sorcerer, just as strange as his name, Ne-sia-Hualala, 'I-will-cry'. What a name to give a child! His father used to be a sorcerer too. But I have never seen anybody perform like him. I didn't like his songs. They always made me feel queer. But he was a fine man and everybody liked him. He was good looking, too. And so was Hualala's mother. It is funny they should have made a child as ugly as he is. Maybe that's why they called him that name, to warn him that he would be unhappy. Well, he is unhappy enough right now. He was crazy about that woman of his. And now he is gone wandering. He started wandering towards the end of last moon. I think he must have lost his shadow. I have come upon him several times in the brush, singing and crying, breaking branches and throwing rocks about, and dancing in the bottom of canyons. Well, you know how a man acts when he starts to wander. It made me awfully sad to see him like that, and I tried to catch him and bring him back to the village. I thought the old blind man might go to work on him and bring his shadow back before it is too late. But he threw rocks at me and ran away."

Both men lapsed into silent contemplation of the sea way down below them and stretching far away to the west, calm and purple with a trail of copper from the sun.

Suddenly, a wild song broke from the woods below them on the other side of the ridge, and both men jumped to their feet. The song stopped as suddenly as it had commenced. There was a silence, then a series of incoherent shouts and the noise of snapping branches.

"There he goes, that's he", said Pawi, and he added: "Oh, it makes my heart sick."

There was silence again. Ruiz said, "It makes my heart sick, too. Let's call him. Maybe he will come." And he let out a calling yell: "YIIIa-a-a-ay-ha! Iyo-o-o, Hualala iyo, miitz iyo! Come Hualala, come my brother!"

There was an answering yell from the woods. Then silence again. "There, he is coming all right, I hear him coming up. Call again."

A man emerged from the woods onto the trail at a short distance from where they were, and stood there hesitating for a moment. Then he saw them and came their way. He had a rumbling, heavy sort of gait, almost a shamble, and yet with something cat-like about it. He was a hunchback with long swinging arms. His face was almost hideous, with one eye gone, and the other red from crying, a huge mouth full of pain, and a wild mass of hair, very long and tangled. He stopped in front of them and started to dance and sing. Then he stopped and sat on his heels, looking at the setting sun. He said: "Well, what do you fellows want, you called me and I came. If you want a doctor, then it's no use, because I have lost my power. I have no power now. I had lots of power, but now it's gone. But I know you two fellows. I know who you are. You are Pawi-maliay-hapa, and that's your brother, the man who stole my woman."

"No I did not, Hualala, you know I did not do that."

"That's right. You didn't do it. It wasn't your fault. I have nothing against you. If anybody says I am going to kill you, it is not true. You can't help it if you are in love with her. I know what it is, I who am her husband. She was so beautiful! She was my power. Now she is gone and she has taken my power away. I have no more power. I could not kill you even if I wanted to. But why should I want to kill you? Because you love her? You can't help that. You did not take her away. She went away herself. I have nothing against you. You can have her for your woman. She is all right. She is a fine woman for a man."

He sat looking at the setting sun. In spite of all his ugliness there was beauty in his face. It was full of malice, and full as well of gentleness. At the moment it was drowned in sorrow.

"Listen, Hualala", said Kinikilali, "why don't you let me buy her from you? What's the good worrying about her. She loved you too, but she was afraid of you. She was afraid of your power. A sorcerer should not have a wife, no more than a hunter. Let me buy her from you. I will give you twice what you gave for her."

"I don't want anything for her", said the young sorcerer quietly. "I tell you, you can have her as a gift. I don't want anything. I can get all I want with my doctoring, if that was what I wanted."

"Don't be silly, Hualala. Listen, I will give you a horse, and show you how to ride, I don't care what the white men say!"

But Hualala flew into a passion. "What do I want a horse for? Am I not ugly enough without showing it to all the world, sitting on top of a horse?"

When he was quiet again he began to cry. "We had a beautiful baby. I am so ugly, but he was a beautiful child. Everybody said to me, 'I like your child.' But she killed it. She says I killed it with my power, but that's not true. She killed it, she killed it by not loving anymore. She didn't love me anymore. How could the child live after that, when it was my child, the child of my love. She took away her love, she took away my power. Of course the child died. My father used to say to me: 'Look at your mother and me, look at us, we have always been happy. That's because we love each other. We don't go fooling around like so many other people. That's the way to do it. You love the woman you buy. She has bought you also. She will love you, and your child will grow. That's the way to do it.' That is what my father used to say. But he gave me the wrong name. He could not help that. He used to say: 'You do what is right and your child will grow straight like a tree.' I guess he loved me so hard that he didn't see that I was all crooked already."

The young shaman began to cry again. Ruiz-Kinikilali cinched his horse and started down the ridge. Pawi went down the other way, towards the Indian rancheria.

Ne-sia-Hualala remained alone, gazing at the setting sun. It was almost in the water, now, huge and red. Hualala looked and looked through his tears. He saw his mother, there in the sun. She had her pack-basket on her back and she was digging for roots, there in the red, huge sun. She did not go out of its circle, but was going further and further away, towards the center, getting smaller and smaller. Once she turned around and looked at him. Her face grew very large, as big as the whole sun, and then she disappeared.

Then he saw his father. He was dancing and singing, right on top of the sun. Hualala could hear the song. It was one of his father's most powerful medicine songs, a song to call back the shadow when it is lost. He saw his father, still singing and dancing, jump into the circle of the sun, and he went away still singing and dancing, getting smaller and smaller, toward the center, and then he disappeared, but he never turned back his head. After he was gone, Hualala saw a little boy standing on top of the sun, right where his father had been. He was playing with a little bow and arrows. He was shooting them towards the water. When he had shot them all, he jumped into the circle of the sun and went away like the other two.

Ne-sia-Hualala sat there looking at the setting sun. He did not see anything else. The sun was half in the water. Now the sun was all gone, and there was the sudden chill of evening. Hualala shuddered. Then he knew that he had seen his own shadow. Then he knew that he was going to die.

He got up and hurried down the trail towards the Indian village. When he arrived there, he went straight to the ceremonial house, climbed to the roof and went down the center-post ladder. It was full of men inside, sitting against the walls, listening to the recital of an ancient tale by Amomuths, the old blind sorcerer. His voice went on and on, monotonously.

Hualala went straight to a pile of bearskins and lay down with his face to the wall. Soon, all the men began to leave silently. They climbed up the ladder, pushed aside the flap over the smoke-hole and went off. You could hear their feet over the roof.

Very soon the old blind man and the young shaman were the only ones left in the ceremonial house. The fire was dying down. The old man kept telling his tale, monotonously, on and on, a long, long tale. When he had finished, he sat in silence for a while. Then he commenced singing a medicine song. It was a shadow calling-back song. He sang for a long time. Then he was silent again. Then he said: "Hey! Hualala! Hey! Ne-sia-Hualala, do you remember that calling-back song of your father's?"

"No, I don't remember it, little grandfather, that was a hard song and he took it away with him."

"That's too bad!" said the old man, and he lay down to sleep.

V. Fray Luis Walks into the Trap and Makes His Bargain with the Devil

Old Saturnino sat in the sun of the courtyard weaving a reata. In the sultriness of the afternoon there were only the small sounds of inactivity. The old mayor-domo sat weaving the strands of raw-hide carefully, methodically, thinking nothing. Then a confused noise in the distance, coming from the valley, the bellowing of cattle, a cloud of dust rising in the air, the vaqueros' yells, and then creeping down over a slope the Mission herd came into view, with a dozen Indians running afoot on either side and behind, and Ruiz-Kinikilali darting everywhere on his horse, shouting commands, cracking his long whip. Old Saturnino ceased weaving for a moment, watching with his mind full of bitterness.

He hated all the Esselens, and Kinikilali particularly. The young vaquero was a tease, and he liked to torment the old mayor-domo whom all the Indians of the Mission feared. He affected to speak of him in the Esselen tongue. "I don't understand that jargon!" the old man would grumble. "Oh! but you ought to learn it, little grandfather, you are not too old yet. I can teach you if you like. Listen, you repeat after me: 'I am an old renegade, I am a mangy old coyote, I am *this* and I am *that*'", *this* and *that* being the two most obscene epithets in the Esselen tongue. The old man only grumbled obstinately: "I don't understand your jargon!"

Saturnino stopped plaiting the strands of rawhide, while he watched the Mission herd and the vaqueros spreading down the side of the valley. Then he resumed his work, waiting for his tormentor.

Now the herd is in the corrals. The gate of the Mission patio swings open. Ruiz dashes in with a gay yell, up to a hitching post, with a swirl and a clatter. The Indians at work making adobes in a corner of the courtyard look up. Some smile, some of them just look with open mouth. Fray Bernardo comes out of his cell, with his eyes full of sleep and a scowl on his face, stands in the doorway a moment, shakes his head, smiles and goes in again. Fray Luis, pacing up and down the arcade, was telling his beads and never turned his head.

But this time Ruiz-Kinikilali was not in a teasing mood. Or perhaps it was that his vaquero's eye, full of thoughts about that bear at the Spring of the Fallen Madronyo, fell in love with the tightly woven reata in the hands of the old mayor-domo. So he came over to him, and squatted on his heels and spoke softly, in

Spanish: "Little grandfather! That's my reata, isn't it?" he begged. Saturnino looked up in sheer amazement. His jaw dropped. "Go to the devil! You... you, oh! you go to the devil!... for you, this reata for you, for you?"

"Oh, for heaven's sake, don't be spiteful, old miser! Can't you take a joke? I don't care a damn whether you are an Esselen witch or a Rumsen apostate, or the head mumbler for the padres! I was just teasing you, that's all. I don't know what you did, except that you killed that woman, and what do I care! She was no relative of mine. Go back or don't go back, just as you like. I don't know what you did. Honestly I don't. They have told me, but I get it all mixed up. Only I don't like it the way you act, denying your own blood, and lording it over us! And anyhow, I won't tease you any more if you give me that reata. Come on now, little grandfather, don't be mean, give me that reata. I want it to get a bear. I must have a reata I can depend upon. You just finish this one for me, and I'll bring you all the bear grease you want. I know you are a bear magician. Oh! what's the use saying no. I don't talk that talk to the padres. I will bring you all the bear grease you want!"

Saturnino did not answer. He never lifted his eyes from the reata. He kept on plaiting the strands of rawhide, desperately. His hands were trembling. He knew he would have to undo all that work, loose plaiting, twisted, not good.

Fray Luis was pacing up and down the arcade, telling his beads.

"Come now, little grandfather, don't be mean! I want that reata. It's just the kind of reata I need. Hold any bear with it. Nobody like you to make a reata, little grandfather!"

Saturnino did not answer. He never lifted his eyes. His hands were trembling. He could not see them very well. He could not think. He went on plaiting desperately. There was something inside of him that tried to work, and would not work, only jerked and hurt, like a cramped muscle. Years and years of pain, of hatred. Hatred of the padres, hatred of the Esselens, hatred of the Rumsens, hatred of a courtyard filled with sun, each day, each day plaiting strands of rawhide, while the breakers boomed on the beach, over there on the other side of the wall. Hatred, memories, years of it, listening in the winter nights to the stormy winds from the south. Cut off from his power. Teaching prayers in Spanish to the neophytes! And now, a little snarling dog biting his legs, little snarling puppy begging a reata, puppy, mongrel puppy daring to tease him, him an old bear doctor, a powerful doctor, that's what he had been.

"Come, little grandfather, don't be mean, you finish that reata for me. Tell me you will. I shan't tease you anymore!"

Saturnino did not answer. He kept on plaiting. Fray Luis was still pacing up and down. The Indians who were making adobes struck up a song. Saturnino felt something bitter like gall spread throughout his whole body. He thought: "That's my power, he will come tonight." He kept on plaiting.

Now Fray Luis has finished his rosary. He hangs it in the monk's cord at his waist. He leaves the arcade. He crosses the patio.

Ruiz-Kinikilali stood up with a curse. He muttered in the Esselen tongue: "There comes the other fox, now, strutting with his tail over his head! All right, you old stubborn piece of rotting meat, I am going now. I want that reata, and I am going to have it, and you had better make it good and strong, otherwise I will...." Fray Luis was now quite close. The vaquero strode off, nonchalantly.

Fray Luis seemed lost in thought. He stopped in front of the old mayor-domo, watching his hands absently. Then he sat down beside the old man.

"Saturnino", he began, "they say that you know more about the old pagan ways than any other of the old men around here. Tell me something that I have been thinking about.... Hey! Saturnino! Listen to me. Are you awake or asleep? I believe you do weave in your sleep!"

"No, Your Reverence, I am not asleep. I am listening. Only I wish you wouldn't ask me those questions. And anyhow, why do you want to know about all those bad things? Look at the good Fray Bernardo. He does not bother his head about the pagan customs. He is a good padre. But you, you are too curious of those bad things. Go and ask the other old men. Don't ask me. I don't think it is right of you!"

Fray Luis laughed: "Excuse me, Don Saturnino, and thank you for the lecture. But do not worry. My motives are excellent. We must all learn about the ways of the Devil in order the better to combat him. And as for the other old men, I have already asked them, but they all say that you know more than anybody else."

"Nonsense!" grumbled the old man. He looked at the reata in his hands, puzzling. He began to unplait the strands of rawhide.

"What are you doing?" asked the monk.

"Well, this work is no good. Have to do it over again. That dirty little mongrel came here to make me angry, and I got angry inside, and I spoiled this part. See, look how it's all crooked. You see, Padre, you must have peace inside to work right. Look at those strands, all crooked! And the very end of the reata, too. Almost finished. About two arm-lengths more. Damn that boy! And now what am I to do? Those strands will never plait straight again, not now that they have been twisted once. The end of the reata, too! You are not a vaquero, Don Luis, so you don't know what it means, but you see, this is the end they wrap around the horn of the saddle. Some say that the end of the reata near the honda is the most important part. But I say: Nonsense! Look at all the vaqueros who have a thumb missing. And where is that thumb? Cut off by the reata! Caught in the turns around the horn. Look at all the vaqueros with a limp. And why do they limp? End of the reata jammed around the horn. Can't turn Mr. Bull loose. Pulls down Mr. Horse. Mr. Vaquero under horse. Leg broken. And whose fault? Who made that reata? Old Saturnino!... No, no, Don Luis, you are not a vaquero but I can tell you that this end of the reata is the important end. And now, what am I going to do? I tell you these strands will never plait straight and tight again.... Oh, damn that conceited puppy! And what do you think, Fray Luis, but he had the impudence to ask me to give him this reata, to hunt bears, he said. Hunt bears! Bah! I hope the bear hunts him, and gets him, too!"

"Tche! tche!" reproved the monk. "You mustn't talk that way, little grandfather. You must not wish ill to anyone.... And, look, I may not be a vaquero, but still I can tell you something about that reata, about making a smooth end...."

The old mayor-domo looked at the monk dubiously. "How?" he asked.

"Plait it around a core. That will make the strands perfectly straight, and the reata even."

Saturnino smiled. "Yes, of course, Don Luis, I know that trick. But it's not nice. I know lots of people make reatas that way, plait the strands around a straight core. Of course it looks smooth and pretty... as long as it is new. But the core always stretches first before the plaited strands, and you get a kink, and that's where your reata is going to break. Still, I suppose I might...."

He looked again at the reata in his hands, absorbed in thought. Then he began to curse once more: "Damn that mongrel! I hope he dies! I don't care what you say, Padre, that boy is bad. He is an Esselen anyhow. They are all like that in his tribe, bad people, witches! You yourself, you don't like him, you know very well you don't like him. Why don't you get rid of him? What's the use of your being a priest then? Our priests, they know how to kill people. You ought to be able to make him die. What's the use of your knowing so many prayers, then? I would kill him myself, but I can't seem to do it! You see, half of him is white. Indian medicine does not seem to catch hold on white men...."

The old man worked himself into a fury, and then quickly subsided again, and now he sat brooding, looking at the reata in his hands, never noticing the amazement and horror on the monk's face. In a corner of the patio, several Indians were mixing mud and straw for adobes. They were singing an endless tune. The afternoon was very quiet. Sky very blue overhead. Fray Bernardo came out of his room, drew a chair near the edge of the arcade to get a better light, and began reading his breviary. A cart came in through the gate, loaded with firewood. The driver sat on the tongue, half asleep, goading the oxen mechanically. The cartwheels made a screeching noise. At last, Fray Luis found his voice. But it was a mere whisper, a hoarse whisper: "Saturnino, Saturnino, are you crazy? What's happened to you? What's the matter with you? What do you mean?"

The old mayor-domo snapped back: "Nothing is the matter with me, Your Reverence! And you know very well what I mean. So why scold me? That boy is going to take your girl away, and you hate him as much as I do, and you know it!"

"I don't understand what you are talking about, Saturnino, I think you are crazy. Sitting here in the sun all day...."

"Crazy nothing! He has had her already, or I am a fool! She wasn't in the nunnery the other night. She was there all right in the evening, when I locked them up, but she was not there in the morning. I told Fray Bernardo. But all he said was: Don't bother me this morning! If we don't get a permit from the Comandante we can't buy anything from the ship that has just come into the harbor from the Philippines, and we have only fifty fanegas of wheat left, and they are full of rice on board, and you talk to me about a puta who slept out of her bed last night! That's the way he talked to me. Well, where was she? Was she with you, eh?"

"Silence! you insolent fool, you insolent old fool! Do you want to get the lash, you the mayor-domo?"

"Go ahead, Don Luis, I don't care! Won't be the first time! Remind me of the old days. But that won't give her back to you!"

"Listen, you old imbecile, listen with both your ears: we, the priests, have no intercourse with women!"

"Well, maybe you don't yourself, but all the other padres do! What's wrong with you, Don Luis? Are you a coya?"

The old man's voice was so full of suspicion that Fray Luis' anger subsided and he burst into laughter.

Seeing the tension relieved, Saturnino grumbled: "Give me your cord, Your Reverence, please."

"Eh! my what?"

"Your cord, please, your cord, that rope around your waist!"

"But what for, what do you want my cord for? I need it myself!"

"I want it for this reata here, Your Reverence, it will make a good core. You gave me the idea yourself."

"I think you are a lunatic, Saturnino. Well, here, take it. You are an old fool. You shouldn't sit so long in the sun. Addle your brains. Poor old fellow...!"

The adoberos were still singing their morose tune. Fray Bernardo whisked over the pages. The sun was near the edge of the wall.

VI. The Unholy Partnership Begins

Old Esteban sat on his stump, in the afternoon sun, watching the ocean below. He heard the corral gate screech, then footsteps around the corner of the house, then footsteps inside the house, then the door behind him opened, and he knew without turning the tall young form in the doorway. He said: "Little son, you have been away a long time, I have missed you!"

"I couldn't help it, Sir. The fathers had a lot of cattle to bring in for branding, and you know, I am chief of the vaqueros, I am now for sure, Fray Bernardo told me...."

"Ah! yes, very good, it is well, it is well." The old man's voice trailed off. His eyes roamed over the sparkling expanse of water, looking for a sail. Then he spoke again.

"Somebody died over there, on the other side of the ridge, in the rancheria, while you were gone. I heard the crying for several nights. They have been wailing for several nights. I wonder who it was. Maybe some relative of your mother. I am glad you have come back."

"I think I know who it was, Father."

"Ah!" said the old man, and his eye roved over the glittering ocean.

He stayed there till sunset, looking over the lonely sea at the foot of the lonely hills, then he shivered with the coming dusk and went inside the house. Ruiz had fried some venison. The old man ate in silence. Then he stretched himself in his blankets against the wall, singing an old tune under his breath, an old malagueña. After a time he fell asleep. Ruiz had gone. It was all silent in the house.

All silent, save for a cricket, several mice, and a very active packrat who was trying to bully them. Through the open door the moonlight came in. The mice were busy, storing grains of wheat in a nest where the last rafter met the roof-sill. They stole the wheat from an open wicker basket in the corner at the foot of the old man's bed of blankets, then they crossed the patch of moonlight in front of the open door, and then jumped onto a box, from there onto the table, and from there scrambled up the corner of the wall to their nest. The packrat had a hoard on a shelf behind the sea chest. At present he was trying to take an onion there. His path ran along a tie in the wall as far as an upright, then through a knothole in the upright, and along another tie, and then onto the shelf. Unfortunately the knothole was too small for the onion. So packrat would turn around, back into the knothole and the onion would be jerked out of his mouth and roll onto the floor. He tried it again and again, stubbornly, and every time he had a chance he bullied the mice as they crossed the patch of moonlight in front of the door, while old Esteban snored and the cricket sang in a corner of the chimney.

The cricket sang: "Tse-dze, tse-dze, tsee-dze-dze! They are crying over there. The night is still, but they are crying over there. Tse-dze! tsee-dze-dze! Some people die, but crickets never die...."

The packrat stopped in the middle of the floor: "Well! I'll be damned...." He addressed the room at large, ignoring the mice: "Some people think they have power, they sing, yes, they sing, well... I could sing too if I wanted to, if I were not so busy. What's the matter with this thing, anyhow? Hey, you, Mr. Mouse, shut up, why can't you be polite, and listen to this fellow's song. He is a good doctor, that's a good song, better listen to it!"

MOUSE: "I didn't say anything!"

PACKRAT: "Shut up!"

CRICKET: "Tse-dze, tse-dze, tsee-dze, somebody's dead, somebody's dead, somebody's dead!"

PACKRAT: "How do you know somebody is dead? Lots of people die. Who is dead, anyhow?"

CRICKET: "He had power! His own power killed him, tse-dze, tsee-dze-dze!!"

PACKRAT: "Aw! shut up, you make me sad. What's the matter with you? Why don't you help me with this crazy thing?... There it goes again!"

MOUSE: "Hush everybody!... Somebody is coming...."

Silence in the house. The snoring of Esteban.

A VOICE OUTSIDE: "Ave Maria purisima! Senores!... Paz en esta casa! Por el amor de Dios, dispiertense! Wake up, wake up, and give asylum to a priest!"

ESTEBAN: "A la Virgen Purisima! Who speaks my tongue...."

Old Esteban scrambles out of his blankets, dizzy with sleep, out into the moonlight. There stands Fray Luis, tall, thin, austere, a dead pine-tree, with his two eyes burning.

ESTEBAN: "Where the devil do you come from? Your voice... your accent...."

FRAY LUIS: "I have been calling for a half-hour! Go and put my mule in your stable, and feed him! Where is your son?"

ESTEBAN: "Your Reverence, I think...."

FRAY LUIS: "Silence, fool! Where is your son?"

ESTEBAN: "I do not know, Your Reverence, my Lord, I do not know. Somebody died on the other side of the ridge, and he went up.... What is it that you want to know, and why do you come at this hour?"

Fray Luis: "You live in an infernal sort of place!... Well, saddle me a horse!"

Esteban: "Saddle you a horse, saddle you a horse!!!! Catch the horse, Your Reverence, and the more luck to you, and be bucked to hell! Who are you anyway? This is your house, and every man and beast is yours, my handsome Lord in your brown skirts, I'll bring you my very best bronco, take off your skirts and ride him, ride him to the hills and to the other side and see for yourself then!"

The two men stood in the moonlight, eyeing each other insolently for a minute. Then the old soldier shuffled away toward the corrals. Soon he came back leading a snorting horse.

"Here, Your Reverence, hold him while I throw my saddle on him. He is young and quick, and a bit snorty, but he won't buck."

"Hurry up, hurry up, old man!"

"But why so much hurry? There is time for everything in this world."

"No, time is short! Death is always around the corner!"

The monk twisted the cassock around his waist and leaped into the saddle. Before starting he turned to Esteban: "You say that the trail is straight over the ridge?"

"Yes, right straight over the ridge and down. You won't have any trouble finding the Indian rancheria. They are holding a funeral dance for somebody who died and you will see the fire long before you get there, and you will hear them singing."

∘ ◎ ∘

Horse and friar were panting up the trail. The moon made the ocean sparkle. On either side of the trail there was a thin mist in the bottoms of the canyons. It rose in curly wisps hugging the slopes, and vanished in the warmer air. Fear was creeping into Fray Luis' heart, and he urged the horse. They paused at last on top of the ridge. A long, lithe, tawny form leaped away and vanished without a sound. A nighthawk boomed close to the monk's head. The horse was panting fast. Fray Luis could feel his own heart beating into his ears. He looked down into the canyon on the outer side of the ridge. Way down below he saw the flare of a fire. Then a waft of wind carried to him for an instant the booming sound of the drum. Fray Luis and his horse started down the trail.

∘ ◎ ∘

Down in the canyon, at the Indian village on the flat, in the moonlight, they were holding the funeral dance for Hualala. From many throats came the song, deep male voices, high pitched notes from the women, a monotonous dirge with strongly marked accents, and a stamping of feet in rhythm.

He-e, hi yan-hiayan, hee... and feet stamping and a whole line of dancers moving as one man, swaying, moving slowly in sideways steps, slowly going around the fire... hee hiam-hee.... And according to the ancient custom, in the ceremonial-house, alone, lay a girl, the handsomest, ready for the stranger, for any who might come....

A VOICE FROM THE TRAIL: "Hermanos! Peace be to this camp!"

KINIKILALI: "Kill him!"

The dance of the mourners has stopped. There is a moment of indecision, while the fire crackles and the trees are illumined. Several men with their hair cropped and their faces smeared with pitch have seized the monk. In the silence Fray Luis' horse whinnies in the darkness outside, then starts home with a clatter of hoofs crossing the boulders of the creek.

FRAY LUIS: "Lord, my God, this is my time, thy will be done!"

THE OLD BLIND DOCTOR: "Who is the stranger?"

KINIKILALI: "A white priest. Kill him."

THE OLD BLIND DOCTOR: "Silence! What do you know! It never was that a stranger was killed at a death dance. Don't I know the way it always was? Take the stranger to the ceremonial-house. The woman is there waiting. Let the stranger take the burden of death from us. That's the way it always was."

An old woman with her hair cropped and her face smeared with pitch jumps up to the monk and executes an obscene mimicry before him. Shouts of ribald laughter. The monk is roughly dragged and pushed to the roof of the ceremonial-house. Shoved through the smoke-hole, with laughter, as he scrambles down the center-post ladder, into the darkness within, and the deerskin flap is pulled over again.

More sticks to the fire. The funeral pyre grows. Tongues of flame leap up curling with dense smoke. An inert body is thrown on top. The old woman sets up the piercing mourning wail, curling high through the night. Other women join. The mourning chant rises again, with the stamping of feet, around and around...

○ ◎ ○

Old Esteban tried to go back to sleep. Then he got up muttering. He saddled his horse, and started up the ridge.............................

The onion rolled onto the floor again for the hundredth time. The mice went on stealing wheat. The cricket sang: "They are burning him at last. He would have been a fine doctor, but his own power killed him. Tse-dze, tsee-dze-dze! Crickets don't die. They live forever like the fire!"

A MOUSE, stopping on his way across the patch of moon-light: "I wonder who the stranger was. Queer looking chap. Never saw one like that before. Something nice about him. I am worried about him."

SECOND MOUSE: "Never mind about the stranger and pack your wheat! The night won't last forever!"

FIRST MOUSE: "Oh! keep quiet! Don't bother me! I wasn't talking to you anyway. You are just a common mouse. You have no power! You don't know anything about that kind. Pack your own wheat and leave me alone. I took a fancy to that stranger. What do you think, Cricket? Shall I go and help him?"

CRICKET: "Tse-dze, tse-dze, tsee-dze-dze! Lots of people die when they are not careful. A man must have a protector. That's the way it always was."

MOUSE: "I am worried about that stranger. Eh, Moon! Hey, Mr. Moon, I want to go up there!"

PACKRAT: "Damn that thing!"

The Moon sends a ray. It comes through the air of night, like a long stick, right through the night towards the open door. It comes to rest on the floor of the cabin. The Mouse jumps on it. They go flying through the night, up, up, towards the mountain.

PACKRAT: "Some fellows are lucky! I wish the Moon would help me with this damn thing!"..

Fray Luis stayed nearly a week at the cabin of old Esteban. The old man liked him, liked to talk to him about the little pueblo of whitewashed houses on the plains of La Mancha. He sang malagueñas, tangos and jotas, in a cracked voice. The monk listened. He was taciturn. They sat in front of the house, in the sun, watching the glittering ocean below. Fray Luis was taciturn and moody. Ruiz was riding the range, gathering stray cattle. He came in only in the evening. He stood in the doorway at their backs and said nothing. They ate venison and acorn soup. Then old Esteban would sing a jota or two and stretch himself on his bed of blankets. Ruiz would walk off to the corral without a word and saddle a fresh horse, and the friar would pace up and down in the moonlight in front of the house, for hours and hours. The nights were warm.

One night he took off his cassock and snatched a wildcat skin for a loincloth, and he started up the ridge. He was excited and feverish. He did not notice the mouse that followed him. He went up the trail fast. He was panting. He got to the top of the ridge. The whole world was bathed in moonlight. He saw a puma slink away in the moonlight. He said: "Brother! help me!" The puma turned his face once and Fray Luis saw the two green eyes for a second.

Fray Luis looked for the down trail. He went down for a score paces. Then he found a bifurcation into two trails. He was trying to remember. The mouse was running down the right trail excitedly and coming back. He would run a little way and come back, and run again, a little small thing, chip-chip-chipping in the mottled light through the trees. But Fray Luis was calling: "Oh, Puma, my brother, come and tell me!" He listened intently in the silence of the night. He was panting. He thought he heard a sound coming, coming.... He listened.... Jingle-jingle-jingle, the jingle of spurs, and the cadence of a horse's footfalls. Jingle-jingle-jingle, they passed by. Jingle-jingle-jingle, diminishing off in the distance..

VII. Fray Luis Tries to Double-Cross the Devil

What were the results of Fray Luis' journey down the Coast for the propagation of the faith? It is difficult to surmise.

He came back in a sullen mood and answered Fray Bernardo's anxious inquiries with ill grace. "They are the worst kind of wild savages, and we cannot do anything with them!" was all he would say, while the Catalan friar wisely nodded and answered: "Didn't I tell you so?"

On the other hand, if we turn to his diary we find nothing but an incoherent medley of prayers, invocations, appeals to all the Saints, and Martyrs, and Virgins of the calendar, mixed with shocking blasphemies and obscenities, showing that at the time his mind was deranged.

∘ ◗ ∘

It was at about this time that Ruiz-Kinikilali also came back to the Mission. He rode every day. He was gathering the summer cattle. There were many new calves. It was very difficult to keep the different brands apart. Ruiz complained to Fray Bernardo that the new settlers on the Monterey side of the hill were letting their cattle drift towards the Carmel Valley. Already he had brought his cousin Pawi-maliay-hapa to help on horseback, and Fray Bernardo had winked at the breach of the rule against mounting an Indian. So now, when Ruiz demanded several more mounted Indians from the Mission to help him, Fray Bernardo threw up his hands in despair: "No, no, no, no, my dear son, you cannot do that. I have enough trouble with the Comandante already!"

"But, Father, we can't bring in the cattle all alone, just two of us on horses, and a remuda of boys afoot panting a mile behind!"

"Oh, my son, my dear son, you are so much trouble! You are a good vaquero, but you are so much trouble!"

So, in the end, Ruiz got his men mounted and brought in a great many calves, many more than the good Fray Bernardo had ever expected. The friar was thoroughly delighted and happy, and when he heard that old Saturnino was weaving a reata for his pet vaquero, he blessed the old mayor-domo and said with emotion: "God will repay you, you old scoundrel, God will repay you for your forbearance. That boy is not bad. Just foolish and young, but a good boy. Make him a good reata. You are a good old man, God will repay you. Make him the best reata you ever made!" And Saturnino grinned, sardonically.

And when a little while after the branding Ruiz said to Fray Bernardo that he wanted to marry the Esselen girl, now that her own husband was dead, the old friar embraced him with tears: "Yes, yes, my son, my little golden vaquero, marry her, that's right, take her for your wife according to the rules of our holy Church, I give her to you, I am sure she wants you. You take her back with you. This is not a good place for her. She has been a great care on my conscience!" And he trotted in great excitement to break the good news to Fray Luis.

Ruiz was crossing the courtyard. Saturnino called him. He threw the reata at him gruffly: "There you have it, and a good one it is! Now, be sure to bring me enough bear grease to pay me for it."

"For me? Is it for me? Do you really mean it, little grandfather?"

Saturnino did not answer. He gathered his strands of raw-hide and went back into the pozoleria. The vaquero shouted after him: "Thank you, grandfather. I will bring you all the grease you want! I'll get that bear now!"

He stood for a while slowly coiling and uncoiling the reata. He was running it through his fingers, amorously. Not a fault, not a kink, not a single uneven place. Like a snake, lithe, coiling and uncoiling. His eyes were large with pleasure. Then he caught sight of Pawi, at the other end of the courtyard, talking to several Indians. His manner changed. Mischief bubbled over him. He slid open the loop, he tiptoed to the group. The other Indians saw him but never betrayed it by even a wink. There was a hiss through the air, and a very small loop descended neatly over Pawi's head. He turned quickly, but his arms were already pinioned with a jerk. Ruiz-Kinikilali "sat" on the end of the reata and danced on one foot, all the while imitating the grunt of a bear. There were shouts of laughter all over the courtyard. Fray Bernardo came out of his cell to see what was the matter, and he laughed.

The sun was halfway down. The shadows were lengthening. A woman started a song in a high voice; behind one of the walls, Fray Luis was pacing up and down the northern arcade. Every time, as he approached the western end, more and more of his long and gaunt form cassocked in brown emerged into the light, up to his neck. But his head remained in the shadow. He turned slowly, and the golden light retreated down his body, till even his sandaled feet were lost in the penumbra. The late afternoon was windless. It was high tide, and from the beach, over there beyond the walls, came the boom of the breakers.

"Well, let's start for home", said Pawi.

"No, not yet, I don't want to go yet, brother, I want to see my girl, tonight."

"Oh! there you are again! Bad business! Well, I am not going to stay any longer."

"What are you afraid of, Pawi? You can go any time you want to. Nobody will stop you. They can't keep you here. You are not a convert. They can't make you stay here."

"I know, I know, Kini, but I don't like it here. I want to go home!"

"All right, very well, brother, go home, go home. I'll start myself in the morning, but I want to see my girl tonight!"

Pawi-maliay-hapa went over to his horse, the one his cousin had given him, and he straightened the saddle blankets. He tightened the cincha. He did everything conscientiously, the way Ruiz had taught him. He swung himself into the saddle. He said: "I wish you would start right now with me, brother."

But Ruiz only laughed: "If you had a girl here, you wouldn't be in such a hurry to go home. Never mind, I'll be there tomorrow and we'll get that bear! Go on now, metele, metele, vaquero!"

He slapped the horse on the haunch and threw up his arms with a yell. The horse was young, and had it not been for two weeks of daily riding, he would have bucked. As it was he only spurted away in a cloud of dust toward the gate. The Indian at his post there smiled, threw a greeting in Rumsen while he opened the gate hurriedly, and the Esselen vaquero passed out in a swirl of dust. The gates closed again.

 o ◎ o

The night was windless. The Mission was asleep. The girl slid over the wall, and Kinikilali caught her in his arms. She was panting with excitement. He kissed her for a long time. Then they slept in a tight embrace, lost in the moonlight, till the cold woke them. She sat up with a start. "I must go, Kini, little Both-ways, you my darling, oh! it was good, Kini, I must go now, help me over the wall...."

"Oh! wait, little Tickly-one, my sweetheart, let's have another!"

"No, Kini, I can't, I don't want another... yes, I would like it, but I am afraid. Listen, Kini, if I am caught, I'll get whipped again. I can't trust that old woman. She said that if I didn't come back before the moon goes down, she would go to sleep and lock the door of the nunnery. She is afraid of Saturnino. I can't help it. Don't be a fool. Do you want me to be whipped again? I only got ten lashes, but I will get the full twenty-five, this time...."

"What are you talking about? Did you really get whipped?"

"Of course I did! Don't you suppose I would stay here all night with you, otherwise? Let me go! Please, darling! No, I don't want to. I tell you I shall get whipped, twenty-five times, yes, twenty-five times, do you want to take it for me?"

Ruiz-Kinikilali stood up in the moonlight, regardlessly. He was trembling. He said at last: "Who gave you the whipping? Did that monk do it?"

"No the old woman did, the one who is in charge of us...."

"Did it hurt?"

"Of course it hurt! Fray Luis was there watching. She was afraid of him, and she laid it on hard!"

Ruiz-Kinikilali was still trembling in the moonlight. He said: "All right, darling, come on, I'll help you over the wall, never mind, we will soon be out of here!"

She did not kiss him. She hesitated: "Kini, my little Both-ways, please don't get into trouble!"

"I won't get into any trouble. Come on, darling, put your feet in my hands, that's right, now grab my hair, can you sit on the wall? All right, good adios, my little louse, my darling...."

Ruiz-Kinikilali stood there in the shadow for a long time. Then he put his foot in a crack of the wall and vaulted over. He slunk along the wall noiselessly. He knew where the cell of Fray Luis was. He stood outside, in the shade of the arcade. He listened. He heard noises, voices, inside the room, a wild, insane idea came into his mind. He trembled again. Then he felt for the handle of the long blade in the folds of his sash.

He stood under the window of Fray Luis' cell. It was set high, just a little higher than his head. He heard voices inside, at least one voice, but he thought there were two. He could not reach the window. He grasped the ledge. His fingers blanched. He dropped down again. He unsheathed his knife and held it in his teeth. He looked around. He wanted a block of wood, something, anything to stand on. In the darkness of the arcade he could find nothing. He did not dare trust himself in the moonlight of the courtyard.

He grasped the window-ledge once more. With his finger-tips blanched, he looked inside, he looked, he looked inside the cell of the monk.

He saw Fray Luis stark naked, utterly naked, with a whip in his fist and alone. Alone, alone, he was, utterly alone he was, the flagellant in his cell, while the blood streaked down his back. And every time he switched the rawhide, every time he groaned, every time he shuddered and begged the Saints for their mercy. And the blood streamed down the back, red, red, impossibly red.

Ruiz-Kinikilali let his fingers go off the window-ledge. He sank to the ground. His mind was reeling. He himself reeled across the courtyard, full in the moonlight. He did not care. He stood there in the middle of the patio, and he vomited. Then he turned towards the chapel. He found the door. He opened it. He went inside. The sacramental light burned, quietly, evenly, soothingly. Ruiz-Kinikilali did not understand, but he prayed.... He prayed, he prayed, and prayed, fervently. He prayed as he stood crouching in the shadow of the pillar: "God Almighty, my Father, my own Father, save me, save me from the Devil, from Him whom I have just seen, my Father, my Father come to me!" Everything reeled before his eyes. A whip lashing through the air. The flesh of a woman, and streaks of red over the white.... Then silence and darkness for a long time..

The door of the Church creaked on its hinges, and the two monks came in for Matins. Fray Luis carried an oil lamp. Fray Bernardo swayed with sleep. Fray Luis lit the tapers. They stood, facing each other across the nave. Fray Luis intoned in a sonorous voice. Fray Bernardo responded, his voice heavy with sleep. Back and forth, back and forth in the hollowness of the chapel. Till the end of Matins. Fray Bernardo put out the tapers. The door grated on its hinges, and closed with a bang. Silence.

Ruiz-Kinikilali shuddered. He looked at the sacramental light. Why should it be red, like blood? He shuddered. He crept to the door, out into the coolness of the night. His horse was tied at the hitching post.

Jingle-jingle-jingle, the cadence of spurs.... Fray Luis turns on his couch and mutters. Jingle-jingle-jingle... off, away, down the road in the moonlight.

∘ ◗ ∘

Fray Luis is tossing about on the planks of his bed. He dreams. He mumbles and moans. He tosses about restlessly and the rough cassock, stiff with blood, tears at the stripes on his back. He moans, while the monsters of the night surge about him in his nightmare. He hears the jingle of spurs. It is dark where he is, and way down there, there is something he must reach, some meeting he must attend. The jingle of spurs in the dark. No, nothing, silence. He must go down there, down the steep trail, dark, dark, in utter blackness, waiting for someone, waiting for her who will lead the way. Ah! there she stands, the black woman, the black virgin, waiting for him by the side of the trail, utterly black in the blackness, she who said: "Nigra sum, sed formosa!" She leads the way down, down, down the dark trail, for a long, for an interminable time. At last they come to the creek. It is a swollen torrent. It must have been raining. She lifts him in her arms. She wades through the water. He clings to her in his fear. There are many people, crowds of people standing in the village in among the huts. Suddenly they all vanish. All is deserted, ominously silent. Still carrying him in her arms, the black virgin, she wends her way in and out of the conical huts (there were thousands and thousands of them). They arrive at the ceremonial-house, large, immense, looming up to the sky. Up to the roof they go, up, climbing to the top of the world. They stand on the roof. He, very small, clings to her, trembling, afraid of her. Down through the smoke-hole they go, down the center-post ladder. Now they stand in the middle of the floor, and all around the wall they are seated, all of them silent, impassive. They begin to chant the mourning song. The black woman has disappeared. He stands there in the middle of the floor, at the top of the center-post ladder. They chant. For whom are they chanting? Are they chanting for him? Is this he, laid there dead across the fire? Or is it the young half-breed vaquero? When did he die? They are chanting, chanting, chanting the death-song, interminably. Will they ever stop? Why must he stand thus, in the middle, without a breech-clout, while they sing around the wall, and the other one burns? He will speak, he will ask for fair judgment. They know it. They stop the chant. He opens his mouth. Vainly, vainly, he opens his mouth. Soundless, speechless, utterly impotent. Why, but why? What is this feeling, abominable, creeping up, up his legs, insistent, anxious, creeping, snatching, gripping, grasping, tearing off, tearing them off, my God!..

The yell sounded through the dawn. Fray Luis lay quivering on the planks of his bed. The first ray of the morning sun came through the high barred window and rested on the opposite wall. A cock crowed. An Indian was yoking the oxen to his cart in the patio: "Hoy! hoy! hoy! aee! hoy!"...

VIII. THE DEVIL CARRIES OUT HIS BARGAIN

Ruiz and his cousin sat in their saddles, in the shadow, at the edge of the little flat where the carcass of a young bull lay, half-devoured, still fresh. It was near the end of the moon, and not much light. They fidgeted in their saddles, in utter silence, shifting from side to side, reatas unslung and the loop trailing to the ground. They dozed and started, and dozed and started, and dozed again. The crackling of a twig, and they sat up in their saddles, utterly awake, impossibly awake, on the very edge of intentness.... Silence for a long time. Maybe the bear had smelled them and gone away.... Then the crunching of bones.... Kinikilali leaned away over in his saddle and placed his lips right into Pawi's ear, so that it tickled him. "Drop your reata! Get an arrow ready. I'll surely get him the way he is placed, and I'll drag him to the south. Get off and shoot while I drag him. All right? All right! Wait.... Ahora!!" And with a yell he rushed his horse in the open. He was left-handed, and as he turned, he swung the loop right over the bear's head uplifted in wonder, and without stopping he circled to the south.

He expected a jerk on the reata, although perhaps not quite such an uncompromising one. The well-trained horse swirled on his forefeet and sat on his haunches. Pawi was there, in the moonlight, just exactly where he was to be. The short, hard bow was drawn way back. The release, and the hum of the string. Almost immediately another arrow. Then another, and a fourth one. Then Pawi stood looking, in the uncertain moonlight, mouth half-opened, with his bow still lifted, with his right arm still drawn back. He had seen every one of the arrows bounce back. And now he was watching the bear drawing in on the reata, arm over arm, slowly, leisurely. At the other end of the reata the horse was plunging frantically.

"Turn him loose, Kini, turn him loose, quick!"

What was the matter with Kinikilali? He was fumbling with the turns of the reata on the horn of his saddle. He yelled: "I am jammed! Shoot him again for heaven's sake!"

Two more arrows. They bounced back.

Down went the horse, on his knees, and Ruiz-Kinikilali tumbled over the horn.

Just a rip of the paw. Then the bear started up the hill, dragging the horse for a few paces, until the reata snapped, near the horn of the saddle.

The bear was climbing up, slowly, leisurely, in the half-moonlight, towards the ridge, dragging the reata....

IX. And Begins to Demand His Price

Esteban sat on his stump looking over the ocean, looking for a sail. After a while he was dimly conscious of someone standing near him. He brought himself to reality with an effort. "What is it, Pawi-maliay-hapa?"

"Kinikilali is dead. The bear killed him."

Esteban's eye roamed again over the glittering ocean. At last he said: "Did he walk away with the reata?"

"Yes."

Esteban sat on his stump looking over the ocean, silent for a long time. Pawi-maliay-hapa stood in silence waiting. Finally Esteban tried to get up. Then he said crossly: "Help me, you!"

They went slowly towards the corrals. "Catch me that horse! No, not that one, this one here, there... bueno... saddle him."

Slowly they rode up the trail, slowly, slowly, because the old man, and he was in the lead, stopped so often and let his head drop, while his horse ate the grasses. But at last they were over the ridge, and Esteban Berenda led the way down the trail, down to the rancheria, and he stayed there a long time with Amomuths, the blind sorcerer...

Fray Bernardo took the news badly, at the Mission, when Pawi came. He wrung his hands and cried and lamented. The adoberos knew already. They had known since the morning of that day, and nobody struck up a song that day, nor for several days thereafter. There was a pall of silence over the Mission. Saturnino sat in the sun in front of his pozoleria, weaving reatas as usual. He was listening intently to the talk between Fray Bernardo and Pawi-maliay-hapa, carried on through an interpreter. Pawi said the Esselens wanted the girl to be returned to them. Fray Bernardo tried to explain that now she had been baptized and was a Christian, she could not leave the Mission any more. Pawi would listen politely, and then repeat his stubborn request: "The old men want her to come back." Until Fray Bernardo went away in despair. He went to seek Fray Luis.

"Here, you know their language, and you have been there. Try to make him understand. I don't want any trouble. My God! I only wish the girl were away from here, but it is against the rules, I cannot do it, I cannot do it. Now, you try to make him understand. These people seem different from our Indians. He just stands there like an idiot, and repeats the same thing over and over again: the old men want her to come back! To the devil with their old men! I can't help it! Fray Luis, you try to talk to him, please!"

And so Fray Luis crossed over to where Pawi-maliay-hapa stood, and spoke to him. But Pawi only looked and never answered, never gave the least sign of comprehension. Fray Luis then made the interpreter repeat what he himself had just said. But Pawi stood there, dumb. Fray Luis reddened and turned back. Saturnino was bending over his reata. Then Pawi went over to him and spoke quickly, in an undertone. Saturnino gave no sign of having understood. Pawi turned and went over to his horse and untied him. He climbed into the saddle slowly. He passed out of the yard slowly. The Indian at the gate opened it, but called no greeting. He closed the gate again...

Fray Luis stopped in front of the old mayor-domo, where he sat in the sun, in front of his pozoleria, weaving reatas. "Saturnino, what's the matter with everybody around here? One would think I am a leper! I am not blind, I can see it! All the old fellows who used to talk to me, they act now as if they were dumb, and deaf. What's the matter? What's the matter?"

Saturnino stopped weaving a moment. Without lifting his head, he said: "I don't know. Who can tell what's the matter with the old imbeciles, they are so old, some of them.... But, listen, Fray Luis, you had better send the girl back!"

"What are you talking about, Saturnino?"

"I say that you must send the girl back."

"But what have I to do with it? Tell this to Fray Bernardo. He has charge of this Mission.... Anyway, it is useless. You know yourself very well that she cannot leave the Mission now that she is a Christian."

"Look here, Fray Luis, I don't want to argue with you.... The girl must go back there, otherwise you and I will pay!"

"Look here, you old addle-brained fool, I don't understand what it is that you are talking about. I am tired of you, and of that girl, and of the Rumsens, and of the Esselenes, and of the whole damn thing!"

And Fray Luis turned away and began pacing up and down the arcade. Saturnino went on weaving reatas..............................

A few days later the Esselen girl disappeared, and Saturnino reported the matter to Fray Bernardo...

Fray Luis wrote in his diary: "Wednesday. Feast of San Geronimo. Nothing has happened today, except that the little Esselen girl has gone. Escaped to her wild home probably. Good riddance, thinks Father Tallow, but it makes me horribly sad. I hear the pounding of the breakers on the beach and it makes me think of her, I don't know why. May God allow that they treat her well, there. I baptized her with my own hands. My one and only Esselen convert! I feel tired and discouraged, these days. I would like to escape too, run away to the wild hills and become a pagan, and adore the trees and the springs and the rocks and get power, as they call it! Nonsense!"...

Two days later they found her body on the beach. As it was not proved that it was a case of suicide, Fray Bernardo had her buried in the graveyard. The next day Saturnino disappeared............

We read in the diary: "I think my usefulness here is ended. Fray Bernardo agrees with me. I am going to write to Mexico and ask to be recalled. The Superiors will surely grant it. Fray Bernardo wants me to carry the letter myself, under the pretext of sending some urgent messages through me. The old Tallow is evidently anxious to get rid of me. Well, I don't care, I am too sick in my heart to resent the old pack rat...."......................................

Fray Luis went out of the gate, leading his donkey, and mounted him outside. Thus he left the Mission, after embracing Fray Bernardo and receiving his blessing. The old man had said, ever fussy and anxious: "Now mind you take the road to the left, and stop tonight at Monterey, and tomorrow at the Soledad, and don't forget to leave that letter there, and then...."

"Yes, yes, yes, my dear Fray Bernardo, I remember all your instructions!" One more blessing, one more abrazo.... Fray Luis went through the gate and now he mounted his burro outside. His long legs were dangling. His head was bent over his breast, thinking and remembering, remembering way, way back, in Sevilla, in Malaga.... The burro ambled along by the sea, along the trail. Fray Luis dreamed and remembered, his long legs dangling....

When he woke up and noticed, they were way down, way down the south coast, where the River from the South opens into the sea. And Fray Luis shrugged his shoulders and muttered: "Why not this way? At any rate, I know this trail! Anda burro!"......................................

X. The Devil is Paid in Full

They rode along the ridge, in the pale light of the very young moon. They rode along the ridge, the donkey and the monk. Along the ridge, along the ridge, in the pale light of the very young moon, southward, southward, to distant Mexico.

They came at last to the cross-trails, the trail to the rancheria, and the monk knew it.

"Hey! burro! where are you going, you idiot?" and he pulled on the reins.

The donkey kept on his way, down, to the left. Fray Luis pulled. He pulled and he tugged. He pulled frantically, but the donkey was on a run now, down, down, down the trail, dark, dark, dark the trail under the trees.

"Hey! burro! Stop, you devil, stop, stop, stop!"

The branches were brushing his face in the darkness. He could hardly keep in the saddle. He grasped the reins. He grasped two antlers! He was riding a beetle, an immense, a gigantic beetle! He slid on its smooth black back from side to side. He grasped the antennae in utter terror.... Down, down, down the steep trail, the dark trail, down, down, down on the black back of the beetle.... They crossed the creek. The rancheria was dark and silent. The beetle climbed to the roof of the ceremonial-house and Fray Luis hung desperately onto the loathsome antennae.

They stopped at the smoke-hole. The beetle looked down. Fray Luis, grasping the antennae, looked down.

There was a small fire burning inside, but there was nobody there except the old Blind Doctor. He was sitting against the north wall of the house.

The beetle scuttled back and Fray Luis slid over its head. He grasped the ends of the ladder. He descended the ladder. He brushed against a reata, nicely coiled, hanging from the center-pole. He went down the center-post ladder.

"Well! here I am, old man, here I am, here I am, here I am!" said Fray Luis. The old blind Amomuths never stirred.

And there they stood, a long time, for minutes, for a quarter of an hour, for almost an hour, looking at each other, the monk and the blind, the sightless old shaman, looking intently out of his blind eyes. The fire crackled fitfully. They sat looking at each other.

It was a long, long time. Fray Luis grew restless. His mind wandered. Sevilla. Malaga.... Yaaaaah! He yelled in his terror. He opened his eyes, he looked, he yelled again, like a child.... The bear! the bear! where Amomuths had been sitting against the north wall... there was the bear, sitting against the north wall.... Fray Luis looked, utterly awake, at the bear sitting against the north wall of the ceremonial-house, and he yelled again....

There they sat, facing each other, Amomuths and Fray Luis, Amomuths against the north wall and the monk with his back against the center-post.

Then it began again, the bear sitting there against the north wall, then Amomuths, then the bear....

Fray Luis jumped up in terror. He could not keep his eyes from the bear-man, the horrible grizzly, immense, immobile against the north wall, sitting up. He felt back of him with his hand. He felt the ladder. Slowly, slowly, he went up, backwards, rung after rung, slowly, never dared he to turn his face.

And then he did. He turned his face. In a panic overwhelming, he turned. He turned around, he grasped the ladder, he ran up the ladder like a squirrel.... He could see the stars.... Their breath was in his face....

Look out, Fray Luis, look out, slowly, take your time... slowly, look out for the reata. It is coiled neatly up there, in true vaquero style, with the loop ready... look out! Look out! Watch for your head.... My God! Don't put your head through the very loop!!!... Ah, there you have done it. Wait a minute! Don't struggle, don't struggle! It will choke you!!! Wait a....

Ah, there you have done it!..

How your gaunt body swings at the end of the reata, Fray Luis! The shadows on the north wall swing, Fray Luis!

Peace be to your soul, Fray Luis.

ACKNOWLEDGMENTS

IN NO WAY WHATSOEVER could this book have come into existence without the generous assistance of Gui Mayo (formerly Gui de Angulo). I only thought of compiling a selection of Jaime de Angulo's writings after meeting Gui Mayo on a visit to Berkeley, in 1998 if memory serves. Gui not only gave me permission to use her late father's writings, but helped at all stages of the project, sending me copies of texts, giving advice and information, and generally encouraging my endeavors.

In addition to thanking Gui Mayo for permission from the estate of Jaime de Angulo to use all the texts in this book, I would also like to credit the following institutions and individuals:

"The Background of the Religious Feeling in a Primitive Tribe," from *American Anthropologist* magazine, is reprinted by courtesy of the American Anthropological Association.

"The Story of the Gilak Monster and his Sister the Ceremonial Drum," from *Alcheringa: Ethnopoetics* magazine, is reprinted courtesy of Jerome Rothenberg.

The Lariat is included by courtesy of the Special Collections, University Library, University of California Santa Cruz (Jaime de Angulo Archive).

I would also like to thank Peter Garland for allowing me to quote some of his own comments from the book he edited of de Angulo's writings and music notations, *The Music of the Indians of Northern California*. This beautiful collection was one of the very first books of de Angulo's I ever came across, and it remains a personal favourite.

Finally, I want to thank my friends John Gibbens and Sharon Morris for reading and making suggestions about my own contributions to this book. Other friends, especially George Touloupas and the late Petros Bourgos, have given encouragement with the project over the past few years, impossible ever to repay.

—*David Miller*

Sources/Notes

Sources

I have mainly intended to provide information on where the texts in this book were located, and to mention some other versions of them. A few additional notes have been provided; the reader is also directed to the Introduction for more information.

I am indebted to Gui de Angulo's *The Old Coyote of Big Sur: The Life of Jaime de Angulo* (Berkeley: Stone Garden Press, 1995), as well as to her correspondence with me. I am also indebted to Wendy Leeds-Hurwitz's "Bibliography" of de Angulo's writing, included as an appendix to *The Old Coyote of Big Sur* (and, in an expanded form, in her book *Rolling in Ditches with Shamans*, Lincoln, Nebraska: University of Nebraska Press, 2004).

First a general note about the texts: Jaime de Angulo often used unorthodox spelling, punctuation, and capitalisation. (As examples of his phonetic spelling, in "Don Gregorio" he has "thoroly" instead of "thoroughly" and "shud" instead of "should.") De Angulo also defended inconsistency in spelling; basically, he felt that it helped to make people see that there was no single way in which a word might be spelled (see *The Old Coyote of Big Sur*, p. 405). I have retained his unconventional spelling throughout. The few changes I have made—mainly with regard to capitalisation—are for the sake of consistency in a given text or where it seems more likely that one is dealing with a typing error in the manuscript than anything intentional. I realise that other readers of de Angulo may disagree with some of my decisions. To give an example with his use of capitalization, in "Don Gregorio" he switches between the capital and lowercase *I* (as in "Both he and i were early risers..." and "I thot she was going to burst into tears"). This is also the case—though to a much lesser extent—in "The Gilak Monster and his Sister the Ceremonial Drum." I've opted for the uppercase *I* throughout. I have also supplied (a very few) other capitals in "Don Gregorio," e.g., "Moorish" in place of "moorish." De Angulo also alternates between "don't" and "dont" (without the apostrophe) in "The Gilak Monster...," as well as using several variants for "Ceremonial Drum" (e.g., "Ceremonial-drum," "Ceremonial*Drum"). Again, I've opted for consistency, using "don't" and "Ceremonial Drum." There are a few instances where hyphenation has been changed, e.g., in *The Lariat,* "mayor-domo" is given by de Angulo as "mayordomo" throughout. De Angulo is inconsistent also in his use of underlining for non-English words. Trying to make this consistent was, however, problematic for more than one reason, especially his tendency to use underlining for emphasis with some non-English words, while in other cases using it where the non-English words don't seem to be emphasized (and in other cases not using it at all). In the end, I chose not to try to iron out these inconsistencies (while substituting italics for underlining). Finally, de Angulo begins a number of sentences in "The Gilak Monster..." with a lowercase initial; I've substituted capitals in these cases.

I've mainly tried to follow the basic format of de Angulo's manuscripts or the original published versions of his writings.

Don Gregorio

First published in Peter Russell's magazine *Nine* (vol. 3, no. 3, London, 1952). It was included in *A Jaime de Angulo Reader,* ed. Bob Callahan, Berkeley: Turtle Island Foundation, 1979. Excerpts were also included in *Coyote's Bones: Selected Poetry and Prose of Jaime de Angulo,* ed. Bob Callahan, San Francisco: Turtle Island, 1974.

"Don Gregorio" was completed in 1949, though de Angulo had attempted to deal with this material about his father and his own childhood at a somewhat earlier date (see *The Old Coyote of Big Sur,* p. 391).

First Seeing the Coast

Published in a truncated version as "La Costa del Sur" in *Coyote's Bones*, as well as in *A Jaime de Angulo Reader*.

This account of de Angulo's first encounter with the landscape of Big Sur was written in the 1940s. The manuscript is untitled; "La Costa del Sur" is presumably Bob Callahan's title, whereas Gui Mayo provided the present title.

The reader might compare the first version of de Angulo's novella *The Witch*, included as an appendix to *Jaime in Taos: The Taos Papers of Jaime de Angulo*, compiled by Gui de Angulo, San Francisco: City Lights Books, 1985. Though vastly different in most respects, these two texts include similar descriptions of the same landscape, and one of the characters in the novella is clearly based on Uncle Al in "First Seeing the Coast."

On the Religious Feeling Among the Indians of California

Published in Willard "Spud" Johnson's magazine *Laughing Horse* (no. 10, Santa Fe, New Mexico, 1924).

De Angulo published a number of other pieces in *Laughing Horse* between 1925 and 1931. (See de Angulo's comments on the magazine, quoted in *The Old Coyote of Big Sur*, pp. 216–217.)

Jack Folsom, whose conversations de Angulo recalls in this piece, appears quite prominently in the memoir *Indians in Overalls* (first published in Joseph Bennett and Frederick Morgan's *The Hudson Review*, vol. 3, no. 3, NY, 1950, and variously reprinted).

The Background of the Religious Feeling in a Primitive Tribe

Published in *American Anthropologist* (vol. 28, no. 2, Menosha, Washington, 1926).

De Angulo published a number of articles and reviews in *American Anthropologist*, as well as in such journals as *Language*, *Anthropos* and *Journal of American Folklore*.

The shaman referred to as Sunset-Tracks in this text is called Old Blind Hall in *Indians in Overalls*, and is also the basis for one of the characters in *The Lariat*.

The Gilak Monster and his Sister the Ceremonial Drum

First published in Dennis Tedlock and Jerome Rothenberg's magazine *Alcheringa: Ethnopoetics* (New Series, vol. 1, no. 1, Boston, 1975). The manuscript is held in the Department of Special Collections, University Library, University of California Los Angeles (Jaime de Angulo Papers).

This text is also referred to as "The Story of the Gilak Monster and his Sister the Ceremonial Drum." De Angulo incorporated it in his radio series, *Old Time Stories*, broadcast over KPFA (Berkeley) in 1949. "The Gilak Monster..." is a retelling of a story he learned from his friend William Benson, a Pomo Indian. De Angulo may well have drafted a version of it as early as 1927. The broadcast version differs slightly from the manuscript (and the printed) text.

The Fury of Loon Woman

Published in *Coyote Man and Old Doctor Loon*, ed. Bob Callahan, San Francisco: Turtle Island Foundation, 1973.

A variant of this text was published (with the same title) as one of "Two Achumawi Tales," collected by Jaime de Angulo and L.S. [Nancy] Freeland, in *The Journal of American Folklore*, vol. 44, no. 172, NY, 1931. (I have no way of knowing how much Nancy Freeland contributed to the version in question.) It was republished as an appendix to *Indians in Overalls*, San Francisco: City Lights Books/Hillside Press, 1990. Another version, again with the same title, can be found in the Department of Special Collections, University Library, University of California Los Angeles (Jaime de Angulo Papers).

The Lariat

First published as *The Lariat* (San Francisco: Turtle Island Foundation, 1974) and subsequently incorporated in *A Jaime de Angulo Reader*. The manuscript is held in the Special Collections, University Library, University of California Santa Cruz (Jaime de Angulo Archives).

This text is also known as *The Reata*. Originally drafted around 1928, it was rewritten sometime after 1943, according to a letter from Gui de Angulo to the present writer (June 11, 1999). The manuscript is held in the Special Collections, University Library, University of California Santa Cruz.

Another version, entitled "Fray Luis and the Devil," can be found in the Department of Special Collections, University Library, University of California Los Angeles (Jaime de Angulo Papers).

Two of the Achumawi shamans de Angulo writes about in *Indians in Overalls*, Sukmit and Old Blind Hall, were used as the basis for characters in the novella. It is also worth comparing de Angulo's individual sketch of Sukmit, "Portrait of a Young Shaman" (*Alcheringa: Ethnopoetics*, New Series, vol. 1, no. 1, 1975, pp. 9–12) with his description of the shaman Hualala in this text.

As I've noted in the Introduction, *The Lariat* is related to two of de Angulo's other novellas, *Don Bartolomeo* and *The Witch*. For *The Witch*, see above; *Don Bartolomeo* was published serially in Gouverneur Morris' magazine *The Independent* (vol. 115, nos. 3923–3926, Boston, 1925), and subsequently as an individual title from Turtle Island in 1974, as well as in *A Jaime de Angulo Reader*.

A few additional textual notes need to be made in relation to *The Lariat*:

CHAPTER III:

"To stamp a chant around a drum under the moon, or to sing a psalm in the gloom of the nave..." The manuscript has "to swing a psalm," which Callahan follows in his version in *A Jaime de Angulo Reader*, p. 116.

"Wake up and open the doors, for here comes the coast from the south!" This is in fact how the manuscript reads, although Callahan's version has "for here comes a rider from the south" (*A Jaime de Angulo Reader*, p. 122).

CHAPTER VII:

Although I've tried to render de Angulo's texts as faithfully as possible, I have changed two pronouns in this section. In the manuscript, de Angulo writes: "Are they chanting for himself? Is this himself, laid there dead across the fire?" Callahan follows this in *A Jaime de Angulo Reader* (p. 160).

CHAPTER VIII:

"He was left-handed, and as he turned, he swung the loop right over the bear's uplifted head in wonder..." I have taken this as an error in typing (with "the bear's head uplifted in wonder" as the correct version), though of course this is open to interpretation. Callahan follows the manuscript in his version of the text (p. 163).

CHAPTER IX:

The manuscript has: "Fray Luis, do you try to talk to him, please!" Again, I've taken this as an error in typing, though without knowing if "do try to talk to him" or "you try to talk to him" was intended. (I've opted for "you try to talk to him.") Callahan follows the manuscript in this instance, too (p. 165).

NOTES

Introduction

1. Peter Garland, in *Jaime de Angulo: The Music of the Indians of Northern California*, (Santa Fe: Soundings Press, 1988), 72.

2. Garland refers to the "brevity, and…the sharpness of one single image" in the poems and the song notations, and refers to thes in terms of "a simplicity that is a return to basics" (*The Music of the Indians of Northern California*, p. 72). "The Fury of Loon Woman," does in fact begin with a song notation, but it is not at all typical of de Angulo's work in this area.

3. Although it is hard to be precise about the dating of some of de Angulo's texts, he was working with American Indian source materials from the 1920s, at any rate. With regard to "later developments," I am thinking especially of the "ethnopoetics" of Jerome Rothenberg, George Quasha and others.

4. The most important source for de Angulo's life history is Gui de Angulo, *The Old Coyote of Big Sur: The Life of Jaime de Angulo*, Berkeley: Stone Garden Press, 1995. This present section is deeply indebted to Gui de Angulo's research. Needless to say, there are aspects of de Angulo's life that I am either barely touching upon or ignoring completely. Readers who are interested in a much more comprehensive account should consult Gui de Angulo's book.

5. De Angulo's eccentric father is the subject of the very amusing sketches in "Don Gregorio."

6. De Angulo's first wife is best known as Cary Baynes (her second married name). She produced the English version of Richard Wilhelm's famous German translation of the *I Ching*.

7. Although de Angulo may well have had as little interest in Jeffers' poetry as he claimed, his relations with the poet and with the

composers Henry Cowell and Harry Partch would surely constitute a fascinating study. I strongly suspect that there were *affini-
ties* there, beyond the purely personal. (There is one letter from de
Angulo to Jeffers in the Harry Ransom Research Center at the
University of Texas, Austin, which does mention his appreciation
of a Jeffers poem, as Rob Kafka pointed out to me in an e-mail of
February 4, 1998. Partch's biographer, Bob Gilmore, informed me
in an e-mail of February 2, 1998 that there was nothing from de
Angulo in the papers of the Partch Estate, and suggested that they
probably only saw each other during the period from autumn 1940
to mid-September 1941—i.e., less than a year. De Angulo's contact
with Henry Cowell, however, was extensive—they met in 1912 and
remained friends until de Angulo's death.)

8. De Angulo had admittedly published a pamphlet, *The "Trial" of
Ferrer: A Clerical-Judicial Murder* (NY: New York Labor News Co),
in 1911, but this doesn't appear to have been a literary effort in any
real sense. For an invaluable guide to his published and unpublished
writings, see Wendy Leeds-Hurwitz's "Bibliography," included as
an appendix to both *The Old Coyote of Big Sur* and *Jaime in Taos:
The Taos Papers of Jaime de Angulo* (compiled by Gui de Angulo,
San Francisco: City Lights Books, 1985). An expanded version
of the "Bibliography" is included in Leeds-Hurwitz's *Rolling in
Ditches with Shamans: Jaime de Angulo and the Professionalization of
American Anthropology*, Lincoln, Nebraska: University of Nebraska
Press, 2004.

9. See *Jaime in Taos*, especially pp. 51–55, 77. Mabel Dodge Luhan
wrote a curiously unflattering account of de Angulo's visit in her
book *Lorenzo in Taos*, NY: Knopf, 1932. (For Mabel Dodge Luhan
and her relations with writers and artists of the time, as well as her
marriage to Tony Luhan, see Sherry L. Smith, *Reimagining Indians:
Native Americans through Anglo Eyes, 1880–1940*, Oxford and NY:
Oxford University Press, 2000.) Robert Duncan's speculation that

Lawrence developed a homoerotic interest in de Angulo would appear to be groundless (see "The World of Jaime de Angulo," Bob Callahan's interview with Duncan in *The Netzahualcoyotl News*, vol. 1, no. 1, Berkeley, 1979—an account which is unreliable or questionable in other respects, too).

10. *The Witch* shares certain themes with *Don Bartolomeo* and *The Lariat;* in fact, the three novellas may be thought of as a trilogy. As with other of his writings, de Angulo produced more than one version of both *The Witch* and *The Lariat.* (Gui Mayo published a version of *The Witch* as an appendix to *Jaime in Taos.*)

11. The exception would appear to be Blaise Cendrars, with whom de Angulo corresponded and for whom *Indians in Overalls* was rewritten (see *The Old Coyote of Big Sur*, p. 391).

12. See *Jaime de Angulo: The Music of the Indians of Northern California* (edited by Peter Garland). Garland reproduces some of these transcriptions, as well as some late musical creations of de Angulo's own, often rendered as highly visual pieces. Garland refers to them as "visual poems," "ideograms of songs we'll never hear" (p. 71). I've written elsewhere: "...de Angulo devised a series of 'songs' that, as much as anything else, are abstract visual configurations of a 'reductive' yet highly evocative beauty" (*Art and Disclosure: Seven Essays*, Exeter: Stride Publications, 1998, p. 31). The reproductions in *The Music of the Indians of Northern California* are all in black and white, but some of the originals of these late pieces are in fact in color.)

13. For the personal reasons, see Gui de Angulo, *The Old Coyote of Big Sur*, p. 295; and for other references to Jaime's later dislike of Jung, pp. 389, 406, 410–411. See also Robert Duncan's comments on Jung in "The World of Jaime de Angulo," pp. 4, 14–15.

14. See Gui de Angulo, *The Old Coyote of Big Sur*, pp. 317–319, 323.

15. This is worth remembering when considering some accounts of de Angulo during his later years—I am thinking especially of Henry Miller's in "A Devil in Paradise." (The text is incorporated in Miller's *Big Sur and the Oranges of Hieronymus Bosch*, NY: New Directions, 1957; see pp. 344–349 for the remarks on de Angulo.) It should also be borne in mind that according to one account at least, de Angulo appears to have refused to take Miller seriously, and often snubbed him (see Gui de Angulo, *The Old Coyote of Big Sur*, p. 376).

16. *The Androgynes* is not as fully developed as some of de Angulo's other fiction, and was excluded from the present collection for this reason. Manuscript copies can be found in the Special Collections at the University Libraries of the University of California Los Angeles and the University of California Santa Cruz. *Indians in Overalls* has been available in various published forms, including as a separate volume from Turtle Island Foundation (San Francisco, 1973) and from City Lights Books/Hillside Press (San Francisco, 1990). Some of the poems have been included in *Coyote's Bones: Selected Poetry and Prose of Jaime de Angulo*, ed. Bob Callahan (San Francisco: Turtle Island Foundation, 1974), and *A Jaime de Angulo Reader*, ed. Bob Callahan (Berkeley: Turtle Island Foundation, 1979). See also Jaime de Angulo, *Three Poems*, Piraeus (Greece): Kater Murr's Press, 2000. It was decided that de Angulo's poetry would be better served in a separate book than included in the present collection; the same was decided regarding his letters. (In fact, *Home among the Swinging Stars: Collected Poems of Jaime de Angulo*, edited by Stefan Hyner, has recently appeared from La Alameda Press in Albuquerque, New Mexico, 2006.) As already noted, de Angulo's work is not always easy to date, but *The Androgynes* was probably first drafted in 1935, and *Indians in Overalls* was written in 1942 and probably rewritten in 1949 (see Gui de Angulo's Afterword to *Indians in Overalls*, p. 107).

17. *What is Language?* was begun around 1942, and was one of de Angulo's main interests in the last period of his life. The book remains unpublished; three versions of it exist, and can be located in the Special Collections at the University Libraries of the University of California Los Angeles and the University of California Santa Cruz. I have not tried to consult any of these manuscripts, as the book lies outside of my own field of expertise as well as the concerns of the present volume. It is highly probable that *What is Language?* is close to Edward Sapir's ideas. I also suspect that it would be worthwhile comparing de Angulo's writings on linguistics with those of Benjamin Lee Whorf, another of Sapir's associates who worked with American Indian languages. (See Benjamin Lee Whorf, *Language, Thought, and Reality: Selected Writings*, ed. John B. Carroll, Cambridge, MA: MIT Press, 1956.)

18. See Lee Bartlett, "The Pound/de Angulo Connection" (in *Paideuma*, vol. 14, no. 1, Orono, Maine, 1985, pp. 52–75), which also prints some of the correspondence between the two men (as well as related correspondence). See also the letters between Pound and de Angulo quoted by Gui de Angulo in *The Old Coyote of Big Sur* (chapters 14 and 15, *passim*). Pound translated one of de Angulo's French poems into English; he included both versions in the appendix to *Pavannes and Divagations* (NY: New Directions, (1958) 1974, pp. 242 243).

19. Peter Garland discusses the tapes of these broadcasts—which are held by the Pacifica Foundation in Los Angeles—in *The Music of the Indians of Northern California*, p. 10. He also provides an index of the musical material in the broadcast tapes (pp. 37–41). A recording of one of the broadcasts—revealing de Angulo's resonant voice and idiosyncratically expressive way of reading—was included as an insert in *Alcheringa: Ethnopoetics*, New Series, vol. 1, no. 1, Boston, 1975. The manuscript of the broadcasts can be found in the Department of Special Collections, University Library, University of California Los Angeles.

20. From a letter to Gui de Angulo, quoted in *The Old Coyote of Big Sur*, p. 395.

21. Subsequently appearing in various editions, *Indian Tales* was first published by A. A. Wyn (NY) in 1953; however, the published version consists of less than half of the original manuscript. Bob Callahan later edited *Shabegok* and *How the World Was Made* (also referred to as *Old Time Stories*, vols. 1 and 2), from the remaining material. ("The Fury of Loon Woman," included in this volume, is related to *Indian Tales*.)

22. Quoted in *The Old Coyote of Big Sur*, p. 235. De Angulo is reporting his own comments to Tony Luhan.

23. From a letter to Ruth Benedict, quoted in *The Old Coyote of Big Sur*, p. 248.

24. His approach to American Indian cultures was in certain instances limited by the dominant European/Anglo-American anthropological thinking of his time. See Peter Garland (in *Jaime de Angulo: The Music of the Indians of Northern California*): "[De Angulo's] use and acceptance of certain concepts of 'primitive' and 'civilized' in regards to these California cultures, is certainly out-dated." But as he also points out, "it is actually quite apparent that de Angulo himself was above such limited and ethnocentric values, but these do once in a while appear as hold-overs in his writings, especially the more purportedly 'scientific' ones" (pp. 11–12).

25. D. L. Olmsted, *Achumawi Dictionary*, Berkeley and Los Angeles: University of California Press, 1966 (University of California Publications in Linguistics, vol. 45), p. 5. Yet as Olmsted points out, de Angulo produced significant scholarly work. Olmsted's Introduction pays handsome tribute to de Angulo, as well as providing an interesting early attempt to sum up his life. His comments on de Angulo's encounter with D. H. Lawrence are also worthwhile.

26. *Indians in Overalls* (included in *A Jaime de Angulo Reader*; see p. 225).

27. See de Angulo's comment to Pound, "after all, the meta-logical thinking is as *valid* as the logical" (quoted in *The Old Coyote of Big Sur*, p. 423). It is instructive to look at what de Angulo says in "The Background of the Religious Feeling in a Primitive Tribe" about the religious character of the Gambling Game, for example, and compare it with "The Gilak Monster and his Sister the Ceremonial Drum." (This is true even though he is writing specifically about the Achumawi rather than the Pomo in "The Background of the Religious Feeling in a Primitive Tribe.") Also, see further in the same essay and in "On the Religious Feeling among the Indians of California," where he writes about the Achumawi's sense of religious or spiritual power (as the "background" of their religious experience). We could compare Rudolf Otto's discussion of the "numinous"—mysterious, awe-inspiring, sometimes terrifying spiritual feelings—in *The Idea of the Holy* (tr. John W. Harvey, Oxford: OUP, 1923, 2nd ed., 1950); however, de Angulo is anxious to distance the Achumawi's religious feelings from any conception of Godhead, while Otto, with his Christian viewpoint, is quick to tie his account of numinous feelings to the notion of God. De Angulo's interest is also more in the psychological aspects of religion, rather than in religion *in itself*—indeed, he doesn't distinguish the religious from the psychological.

28. To give another example, he ends *Indian Tales*, which of course is also based on traditional American Indian narrative material, with an audaciously self-reflexive turn, handled in a playful way (*Indian Tales*, Berekley/Santa Clara: Santa Clara University/Heyday Books, 2003, pp. 234–236). For *Indian Tales*, see Darryl Babe Wilson's Foreword to the Santa Clara University/Heyday Books edition; and see also my essay "The Dark Path," Charleston, Illinois: tel-let, 2000.

29. Wendy Leeds-Hurwitz's study of de Angulo is indeed entitled *Rolling in Ditches with Shamans.*

The Background of the Religious Feeling in a Primative Tribe

1. This is a verbal infinitive: *samagoma,* I poison; *kamagoma,* you poison; *yamagoma,* he poisons; *damagomi,* to poison; *itu damagomi,* my poison, etc.

2. Also a verbal substantive, from the root $\sqrt{ho}$, the exact meaning of which is "to be sacred," "to be non-ordinary."

3. The damagomi referring to the shaman says "my father," while the dinihowi calls the man he favors "my brother."

4. I cannot help giving a hint of the wealth of material that lies here for the student of analytical psychology. The very much respected Marumbda is the lineal descendant of the fool Coyote, while the remote Kuksu with his enigmatic bird head is the introverted Grey Fox. Fox was always chiding Coyote for protean restlessness. But Marumbda could never have created the world unless Kuksu had given him the substance out of his armpits. The whole enigmatic tale needs treatment, and by real scientists.

Printed in the United States
by Baker & Taylor Publisher Services